KRISTY THOMAS,
DOG TRAINER

**Other books by
Ann M. Martin**

P.S. *Longer Letter Later (written with Paula Danziger)*
Leo the Magnificat
Rachel Parker, Kindergarten Show-off
Eleven Kids, One Summer
Ma and Pa Dracula
Yours Turly, Shirley
Ten Kids, No Pets
Slam Book
Just a Summer Romance
Missing Since Monday
With You and Without You
Me and Katie (the Pest)
Stage Fright
Inside Out
Bummer Summer

THE KIDS IN MS. COLMAN'S CLASS series
BABY-SITTERS LITTLE SISTER series
THE BABY-SITTERS CLUB mysteries
THE BABY-SITTERS CLUB series
CALIFORNIA DIARIES series

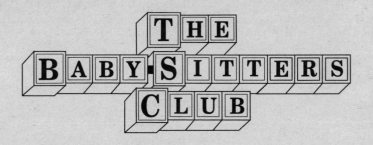

KRISTY THOMAS, DOG TRAINER

Ann M. Martin

AN
APPLE
PAPERBACK

SCHOLASTIC INC.
New York Toronto London Auckland Sydney

Special thanks to:
Michelle Saunders
Anne Aldrich

Cover art by Hodges Soileau

No part of this publication may be reproduced in whole or in part, or stored in a retrieval system, or transmitted in any form or by any means, electronic, mechanical, photocopying, recording, or otherwise, without written permission of the publisher. For information regarding permission, write to Scholastic Inc., Attention: Permissions Department, 555 Broadway, New York, NY 10012.

ISBN 0-590-05996-3

12 11 10 9 8 7 6 5 4 3 2 1   8 9/9 0 1 2 3/0

Printed in the U.S.A.   40

First Scholastic printing, April 1998

*The author gratefully acknowledges
Nola Thacker
for her help in
preparing this manuscript.*

KRISTY THOMAS, DOG TRAINER

CHAPTER 1

"Hey, Watson! Isn't it a great day? Want some more coffee? It's decaf, right?" It was the first Saturday in April, and it *was* a great day. I'd gotten up early to find Watson, my step-father, sitting at the kitchen table, a coffee mug in one hand and what I thought were gardening catalogs spread out on the table around him.

Watson and my grandmother, Nannie, who also lives with us, are the gardening gurus of Stoneybrook. They'd been poring over gardening books and catalogs all winter — making lists, drawing up diagrams, and throwing around phrases like "soil acidity" and "companion planting."

Don't ask me what any of this stuff means. *I* don't know. But it made sense that on a perfect April morning, Watson would wake up super-early to put in some extra gardening time.

"More coffee would be nice," he told me.

1

"And yes, it's decaffeinated. I *am* following doctor's orders, Kristy, don't worry." The corners of his eyes crinkled in a smile.

I smiled back as I poured the coffee. Watson had a mild heart attack a little while ago, so he has to watch what he eats and does. I made myself some cereal with bananas and honey, fixed a couple of pieces of toast, and sat down at the table.

"Big gardening plans?" I inquired.

"Yes. Nannie and I have been talking about the possibility of a water garden," Watson answered.

"You mean, like a pond?"

"More like a small pool."

I gestured at the brochures without really looking at them. "Water gardens made easy, right?" I guessed. "Will the pool include ducks?"

"No ducks. The pool will be too small for that. Maybe a few fish." Watson took a sip of coffee, watching me over the rim of his cup. Then he added, "But these aren't gardening magazines. As a matter of fact, they're from the Guide Dog Foundation. Your mother and I are thinking of getting a dog from them."

Another dog! I love dogs, but my family is pretty big already.

My name is Kristy Thomas. I'm thirteen years old and I live in Stoneybrook, Connecticut, where I go to Stoneybrook Middle School (SMS), coach a little kids' softball team called Kristy's Krushers, and am president of the Baby-sitters Club (more about that later).

I'm also a member of a very large blended family. Watson is Watson Brewer. He is, as you know, my stepfather. He's also the CEO of Unity Insurance. When he had his heart attack, it made me realize just how important he is to me, which is why I'm a little, well, bossy about his sticking to what the doctor tells him.

But then, bossy comes naturally to me. I have two older brothers, Charlie (age seventeen) and Sam (fifteen); a younger brother, David Michael (who is seven); two younger stepsiblings who live with us part-time, Andrew (four) and Karen (seven); and a Vietnamese baby sister, Emily Michelle (age two and a half). Out of all these people, I think it's safe to say that I'm seen as the bossiest.

I don't think of it as being bossy, though. I call it being organized and getting results. When I take charge, I know things are going to get done, and that they're going to get done the right way.

My mother is even more organized than I am, which is one of the reasons she managed to keep our family together in the tough years after my father left us, back when David Michael was just a baby. Nannie is also strong-willed —

3

when Emily Michelle was adopted, Nannie insisted on moving in with us to help out. Also living with us are: Boo-Boo, the cranky cat; a Bernese mountain dog puppy named Shannon; assorted goldfish, and a part-time hermit crab and rat. We also have a resident ghost (or so says my very imaginative stepsister, Karen).

With all these people and animals in the family, I couldn't see why we would get another dog — unless it was for some very good reason.

"Another dog?" I blurted out. "For us?"

"Slow down, Kristy." Watson told me, smiling. "It's not for us. Actually, Laurel Cooper is the one who got me started on this. She's in our public relations department. Her daughter, Deb, is twelve. She's in the seventh grade at Stoneybrook Day School. Or will be, when she gets back to school."

I knew who Deb Cooper was. My friend Shannon Kilbourne, who also goes to SDS, had told me what had happened to her. A few months ago, Deb had gotten very sick and had lost her eyesight. She had come down with something called glaucoma.

According to Shannon, Deb hadn't been back to school since it had happened. She also refused to allow any of her old friends to visit.

I looked again at the brochures on the table. "You're getting a guide dog for Deb?" I asked.

Once again, Watson had to slow me down.

"Not at all. Deb isn't old enough to have a guide dog, even if she were ready for one. And I don't think she is yet. Because of what happened to Deb, Mrs. Cooper had the idea that our company should sponsor a guide dog through the foundation. The more I heard about it, the more I wanted to get personally involved. So I've been talking to the foundation about becoming a puppy walker."

This time, I didn't jump to conclusions. I finished my cereal and nodded. "A puppy walker?"

"A puppy walker family takes a guide dog puppy and raises it from the time it is eight weeks old until it is fourteen months old. Then it goes back to the foundation for training to become a guide dog," Watson explained.

"Sort of like being foster parents," I said.

"Something like that."

"Cool. When do we start? What kind of puppy will we get? Do we get to choose? Do we —"

Watson laughed out loud. "We have to be interviewed first. Someone from the foundation will be here next Wednesday, assuming that everyone in the family agrees it's a good idea. If the foundation decides we'll make a suitable family, we'll go from there."

"I vote yes," I offered enthusiastically. "I think it's a great idea."

Just then, Nannie came into the room.

"We're getting another dog!" I announced.

"So I heard," she answered. Obviously, the adults in our family had already discussed the issue.

"I'll talk it over with your brothers and sisters today," Watson said. "And we can all discuss it at dinner. Needless to say, it's a family decision."

"I don't need to talk it over. As I said, you've got my vote," I reminded him.

"I thought I might. You know what? You're my favorite thirteen-year-old daughter," Watson joked.

"I'm your only thirteen-year-old daughter," I said, blushing a little in spite of myself.

"And I wouldn't have it any other way," he added lightly.

"Me neither," I said. Then, before we could all get *way* too sentimental, I asked, "If our dog is a retriever, can it go swimming in our water garden?"

Nannie said firmly, "I don't know what all the rules are for raising a guide dog puppy, but this rule applies to all dogs everywhere: No canines allowed in the garden!"

"That," I retorted, "is a doggone shame."

CHAPTER 2

"Tell me, tell me, tell me," Claudia Kishi begged.

"Not until everyone gets here," I answered.

"These cookies," said Claudia, "are home-baked chocolate-chip cookies. My mother brought them home from the library fund-raiser. Her assistant made them."

Mrs. Kishi is the head librarian at the Stoney-brook Public Library. Her assistant's chocolate-chip cookies were famous all over town. I held out a hand.

"Nope," Claudia said sweetly. "Not until everyone gets here."

I groaned. "Okay, I'll swap you a clue for a cookie."

"Animal, vegetable, or mineral?" Claudia asked.

"Animal."

Claud paused. She thought hard. She said, "Shannon is going to have puppies?"

"No! Shannon's a puppy herself! Plus, too many people let their dogs have unwanted puppies. You know, animal overpopulation is a *huge* problem."

"All right, all right!" Claudia held out the bag. "Take one."

I'd just bitten into the perfect combo of chip and cookie when Mallory Pike and Jessica Ramsey came into the room.

Claudia glanced at them, remembered their shared passion for horses, and asked me, "Is it a horse?"

"Who's getting a horse?" Jessi wanted to know.

"No one," I said.

"I'm *not* pet-sitting a horse," said Stacey McGill, who had run up the stairs behind Mal and Jessi.

"A horse?" I heard my best friend, Mary Anne Spier, say from the hallway, in a faintly alarmed voice. "We've got a horse-sitting job?"

"A horse-sitting job?" Abby Stevenson followed everyone else into the room and fell back across Claudia's bed. "Does that mean we have to sit *on* the horse? Nah. We don't sit on babies, even though we're baby-sitters."

"Feeble," I told Abby, who makes the worst puns and jokes in the entire universe. "This is how rumors get started. There is no horse. But there *is* a dog. And I'll tell you all about it as soon as this meeting of the BSC comes to order."

"So call it to order," said Abby. "I don't know how much longer we can hold our horses."

As everyone (but Abby) groaned, I glanced at the clock on the desk. Five-thirty on the nose. "This meeting of the BSC is now in session," I announced.

Claudia, Mary Anne, Stacey, Mal, Jessi, Abby, and I are the seven main members of the Baby-sitters Club. I founded the club awhile ago, before Mom married Watson. The brilliant idea for the club came to me one Tuesday night as I sat and listened to Mom call one baby-sitter after another trying to find someone to watch David Michael. *What if Mom could make just one little phone call*, I thought, *and reach several baby-sitters at once?*

I enlisted Mary Anne, who lived next door to me at the time, and Claudia, who lived across the street. Together with Stacey, we started the club.

The idea was such a good one that we quickly expanded. Now the club has more than doubled its original size to include not only seven regular members but also two associate members (who don't have to attend our meetings) and an honorary long-distance member who lives in California. We've been so successful that we have more than enough business from regular clients, who call us often, and new clients to whom our regular clients recommend us.

We meet three times a week, on Monday, Wednesday, and Friday afternoons from five-thirty until six. Clients know they can call us at that time to schedule sitting jobs. Mary Anne, who is our secretary, keeps our record book. She enters all our scheduling information (such as Jessi's weekly ballet lessons) and our baby-sitting jobs into it. She has never, ever made a mistake.

We also have a BSC notebook, in which we write up what happens on each job. Every BSC member is responsible for keeping the notebook up-to-date. Some of us, like Mal, enjoy writing about the sitting jobs. The rest of the members think it's a big pain. But we all enjoy reading it, and it helps keep us on top of what's going on with our BSC charges. We also use the notebook as a reference when we have problems on similar jobs — it's useful to see how other BSC members have handled the same type of experiences.

We collect dues every Monday. That's Stacey's department. She's our treasurer. We use our dues for incidental expenses, such as Claudia's phone bill (she's the only BSC member to have her own private phone line, which is why we meet at her house and one of the reasons she's our vice-president), gas money for my brother Charlie (who gives Abby and me rides to our meetings), the occasional pizza party and special project, and additions to our Kid-Kits.

Kid-Kits, as I have said many times, are our secret weapons in the war on kid boredom and fear of a new baby-sitter. We each have our own box with kid-friendly items — old toys, puzzles, games, and books, plus stickers, markers, and more. We usually take the Kid-Kits along on jobs with new clients because they are great icebreakers, or when we sit for kids who are maybe a little stir-crazy from bad weather or illness.

My Kid-Kit is small, but it's packed with fun things. In many ways, this reflects who I am. I'm the shortest person in the BSC, which is not surprising, since I'm the shortest person in the eighth grade at Stoneybrook Middle School. Even Jessi and Mallory, who are in the sixth grade, are taller than I am. I have medium-length brown hair, pale skin, and brown eyes. I wear jeans and sneakers almost all the time.

Jessi and Mallory are junior members because they are eleven years old and can't baby-sit at night during the week, unless they're sitting for their siblings. Jessi and Mal are best friends. In addition to their love of horses, they also share a love of mysteries and

11

of Marguerite Henry books (which are mostly about horses).

Mallory is shorter than Jessi. She has reddish-brown hair and pale skin with a dusting of freckles. She wears glasses and has braces, to her eternal despair. Like me, she's casual about her clothes. She wants to be a writer and illustrator of children's books and has already had a job working for Henrietta Hayes, a famous author who lives right here in Stoneybrook. Mal has also won an award for her writing. We're sure we'll see her name on a best-seller list someday.

One of the reasons Mal is such a good writer is because she's got a million good stories to tell. In her very large family Mallory is the oldest of eight siblings. When you have that many brothers and sisters, including triplet brothers, wild and crazy things can (and do) happen. Not only has this given Mal lots of material for stories, but it has given her lots of experience staying calm when the unexpected happens — an invaluable trait in a baby-sitter.

Jessi's the oldest in her family, but she has only one younger sister and one baby brother. Jessi has dark brown eyes, brown skin, and black hair that she often wears pulled into a dancer's knot at the nape of her neck. She has a dancer's strong, graceful build, which is a good thing, since she wants to be a professional ballet dancer.

Jessi is *very* serious about her dancing. Not only does she take ballet lessons twice a week with a special teacher, but she also gets up at exactly 5:29 every morning to practice at a *barre* her family has set up for her in the basement of their house. Even her fashion choices reflect her love of ballet. She often wears one of her many leotards with a pair of jeans.

Another set of best friends in the BSC are Claudia and Stacey. They share a keen fashion sense, but Stacey's style is more magazine-sleek, while Claudia tends toward the funky and the far-out. Both Stacey and Claudia are tall, slender knockouts, but they look very different.

Stacey is blonde, with blue eyes and pale skin. Even though it was April, she wasn't wearing spring colors at our meeting. She had on black jeans, a black cropped cotton sweater, and soft, scrunchy ankle boots. The color made her blue eyes look dramatic, and her earrings, which were tiny coils of gold braid, finished the outfit. Even to my inexperienced eye she looked sophisticated and smashing.

Plus, she looked as if she were slightly older than the rest of us. She isn't, but in some ways she's more worldly and a bit more grown-up.

Part of this is because she's from New York City originally. (Her parents are divorced and her father still lives there. She visits him often.)

Stacey is also diabetic. Because of this, her parents were super-overprotective of their only child, and Stacey has had to work hard to convince them that she could be responsible about managing her condition. This means that she has to be very careful about what she eats (no sugar or sweets, or she might get really sick), and she has to give herself insulin injections regularly (ouch). It's a big responsibility, but one that Stacey seems to take in stride, accepting it as something that's no more remarkable than her amazing math abilities.

Yes, math abilities. I'm good at math, but Stacey *loves* it. She actually enjoys books about economics, and can work out compound fractions, for example, in her head.

Claudia, on the other hand, is not a math whiz. In fact, she's a pretty mediocre student, so much so that her parents try to go over her homework with her every night. From time to time she also works with tutors at school.

Her total lack of industry in the grade grind mystifies Claudia's parents (don't forget, her mother is a librarian). It doesn't help that Claudia's older sister is a genius who takes classes at the local college even though she's still in high school.

Claudia's a genius too, but a rarer sort of genius. She's an artist and she sees the world not in numbers or words, but in colors and shapes and textures. Even junk food, one of Claudia's passions (she keeps supplies of it hidden around her room and provides us with nourishment at our meetings), has furnished material for her artwork.

As an artist, Claudia is often her own best canvas. Today she was wearing spring on her sleeves, almost literally. Her ensemble included a giant Hawaiian print shirt worn over hot-pink bicycle shorts, hot-pink-and-lime-green socks, and an ancient pair of formerly black Doc Martens that she had painted in swirls of electric color. She'd knotted a pink plastic flower into each shoelace and had pulled her hair back with another pink plastic flower. Her earrings, which of course she'd made herself, were dangling sprays of tiny pink, green, and yellow beads.

If it sounds blinding, it was. But on Claudia, with her perfect skin, dark almond-shaped eyes, and straight black hair, it was also stunningly right.

Mary Anne and I are the other set of best friends in the BSC. Mary Anne is also short (but yes, taller than I am) with brown hair, pale skin, and brown eyes. She's a fashion conservative, but she does *not* wear the same kind of clothes every day as I do.

Like me, Mary Anne is part of a blended family. Her mother died not long after Mary Anne was born, and Mary Anne can barely remember anything about her. Mr. Spier raised Mary Anne all alone, and he was a loving but very strict parent, because he didn't want to make any mistakes. That was okay, until Mary Anne wanted to stop wearing pigtails every day and pick out her own clothes.

After a bit of a struggle, her father realized she was growing up and he relaxed a little. Then his old high school sweetheart, Sharon Schafer, who'd recently been divorced, moved back to Stoneybrook with her daughter and son.

Mary Anne became best friends with Dawn Schafer, who had transferred into SMS. (At first, I had a hard time admitting that my best friend could have two best friends. But Mary Anne and I sorted that out.) Dawn joined the BSC as an alternate officer. When Dawn's mother and Mary Anne's father were married (with a little help from Dawn and Mary Anne), Mary Anne and her father and Mary Anne's kitten, Tigger, moved into Sharon and Dawn's old farmhouse.

Mary Anne is almost painfully shy and sensitive — even touching commercials can make her cry. She's not nearly as outgoing and outspoken as I am. Dawn is somewhere in between. She can be as stubborn as Mary Anne or me. She's outspoken about what she believes in, such as recycling, vegetarianism, and being environmentally responsible.

Dawn is tall and thin and very blonde, with pale blue eyes and pierced ears, two holes in each ear. She's not the sports fanatic that I am, but she's an avid surfer (her skin tans easily and even catches a few freckles from the sun). Surfing was probably one of the reasons she missed California so much. In fact, both she and her younger brother ultimately made the very difficult decision to move back to California to live with their father.

That's how Dawn became an honorary member of the BSC. She still visits often and we all stay in close touch. We've even been known to trade cross-country advice on baby-sitting.

Finding an alternate officer to replace Dawn wasn't easy, until Abby, our newest member, moved to Stoneybrook from Long Island with her mother and her twin sister, Anna. Like me, Abby is outspoken (too outspoken sometimes — she even argues with *me*) and a sports fan. But she takes it a step further. She's a soccer star and is always in training for something.

17

(That afternoon, she'd come straight to the BSC meeting from a pick-up soccer game.) I don't think she ever walks if she can jog. As Abby would tell you, she has fast feet and a fast mouth — her idea of a joke, just proving my point that she also has a weird sense of humor.

Abby has a soccer player's compact build. She's medium tall, with brown eyes and curly dark brown hair. She wears glasses or contacts, depending on her mood (and sports schedule). Like Stacey, Abby has to deal with health problems. In her case, they're allergies *and* asthma. When Abby says, "Life makes me sneeze," she's not kidding. She has to carry a prescription inhaler with her at all times, in case she has an asthma attack. It's sort of a little tube full of medicine that you breathe in. But Abby doesn't let that slow her down. She lives at warp speed, which is one of the things that makes her a good baby-sitter. She hasn't met a kid yet with whom she can't keep pace.

Logan Bruno, one of our associate members, is the only male member of the BSC. He shares Abby's and my love of sports. Logan is from Kentucky. He has a soft southern accent and he's easygoing and a good listener, a valuable trait in anyone (I appreciate qualities in other people that I myself don't necessarily have). He's also connected to the BSC in another way — he's Mary Anne's boyfriend.

Shannon Kilbourne is our other associate member. She doesn't attend many BSC meetings because she's already booked to the max. She goes to Stoneybrook Day School with her two younger sisters. She's a member of the French Club, the Astronomy Club (where she's the youngest member *and* the vice-president), the Honor Society, and the debate team. She also takes part in most of the school plays. She has blonde hair, blue eyes, and prefers a casual style of dress when she's not in her school uniform.

And that's the BSC — every regular member of which was looking at me now, waiting to hear my dog story.

I cleared my throat importantly.

"Watson wants to raise a guide dog puppy," I began.

"A puppy," said Mary Anne, clasping her hands together. "I love puppies."

"What kind?" asked Abby.

"When?" asked Jessi.

"Is it for someone?" asked Mallory. "I mean, aren't guide dogs the dogs that blind people use?"

Before I could answer any of their questions, the phone rang and we spent several minutes setting up baby-sitting appointments with clients. One of the clients was Mrs. Cooper, who wanted someone to sit for her two sons.

"Deb will be with me," Mrs. Cooper added. After I hung up the phone, Abby said, "Ahhhhh. I get it. Deb Cooper. Is that what this guide dog thing is about?"

"She's home now, isn't she?" Claudia asked.

"Anna said that Shannon told her Deb isn't back in school yet, though," Abby added. (Abby's sister, Anna, and Shannon have become good friends.)

"Deb's the one who inspired Watson to think about raising a puppy," I said. "But the puppy's not for her, of course." I went on to tell everyone about my conversation with Watson.

"We're going to be interviewed on Wednesday," I concluded. "If we pass, I guess we get a puppy."

"We can help you with the puppy," Mallory offered.

"Just tell us what to do," Jessi volunteered.

Mary Anne said in a choked voice, "But it'll be so hard to give up a puppy you've raised."

"I know," I replied quickly. It was something I didn't want to think about. "But we haven't gotten the puppy yet."

"You will," Stacey assured me. Then she held up her dues envelope. "Meanwhile, it's Monday, and I think you know what that means. Payday."

As we handed over our dues, Stacey said thoughtfully, "You know, one of the things that blind people have to learn is how to tell coins apart by feeling them."

Instinctively, I closed my eyes, trying to identify the coins in my hand. The ridged edges meant it was a quarter, didn't they? Or was that a nickel? A quarter, I guessed. Dimes are thinner and smaller than pennies, but was I holding a thin, small dime, or a penny? A dime, I guessed.

I opened my eyes and stared down at the change. I'd been right about the quarter, wrong about the dime. It was a penny.

And what about paper money? I would have no way to know what denomination it was. I'd have to trust others to be honest.

Suddenly, I didn't like this game. And it was only a game for me. It wasn't real.

Not like it was for Deb. I stared down at my fistful of change and realized that I couldn't begin to imagine what Deb was going through.

CHAPTER 3

We passed the dog test. It wasn't easy. Not that we had to fill out a real test or anything (although I know Watson had to sign forms and things like that). I also found out that raising a guide dog puppy isn't quite the same as raising a regular puppy like Shannon.

The test consisted of a visit from a staff member at the Guide Dog Foundation. Her title was Puppy Coordinator, and her name was Gillian, and she was really nice. I liked her the moment she walked into our house that Wednesday afternoon.

We sat in the den for most of the interview. Gillian was very direct and straightforward and let us know from the beginning that the rules for raising a guide dog puppy were in many ways different from the rules for raising a family pet.

"Your puppy is being trained to do an important job," she explained. "It's what she or

22

he has been bred to do. If you don't follow the rules for raising your guide dog puppy, then that puppy will have a very hard time passing guide dog training and won't be able to do the job she or he was bred to do."

I glanced at Karen. Her blue eyes were big and intent behind her glasses. She raised her hand as if she were in school.

Gillian smiled at Karen. "You don't have to raise your hand, Karen. Do you have a question?"

Nodding and lowering her hand, Karen asked, "But what happens if a puppy fails its training? What happens to the puppy?"

"That's a good question. Sometimes the dogs go to work for the police department, or even the customs agency, to be trained to work for them. But if they haven't got the right personalities for that kind of work, the dogs can go back to live with their puppy trainer families. That happens sometimes."

"Oh," said Karen. She looked relieved.

Gillian met all the pets in our family. She laughed when Boo-Boo hissed at her. "Your puppy will learn to respect cats, I see that." She nodded in approval at our yard, which is surrounded by an invisible electronic fence. "That's something that every responsible dog owner should have. It's criminal, in my opinion, to tie up a dog in the backyard, or worse, let it roam loose." Gillian told us then that our puppy couldn't just be let out into the backyard to relieve herself. Instead, the puppy would have to be taught to go on the pavement, on leash, on the command "Get busy," because that is the command that would be given by the blind person with whom the puppy would one day work.

Gillian squatted down to pet Shannon. "What a good girl," she said, laughing, as Shannon licked Gillian's chin and wagged her tail furiously.

As she petted Shannon, Gillian reminded us that our puppy couldn't sleep in the same place as Shannon, or play too much with her, or become too attached to her. "Your puppy has to be people-oriented, because that is who she is going to spend her life with. She can't see another dog and think of it as an opportunity to play. That could be disastrous for her person."

Watson explained that he would be the person primarily responsible for the puppy. "I'll keep a crate in my home office," he said. "As well as by my side of the bed." (When our puppy became a guide dog, she — or he — would sleep next to her person's bed.

There were other rules too. The puppy could chew on balls, but she could never learn to chase them, for the same reason that she couldn't think of every other dog she met as a playmate. She couldn't be fed from the table either, which wasn't a problem. Watson and Mom have been strict about not feeding pets from the table. Mom says it isn't right to teach a dog bad manners and then blame the dog for behaving badly.

And, of course, when a guide dog goes into a restaurant, it can't expect to get a handout from the table!

Those were just a few of the rules. Raising a guide dog puppy was going to be even harder than I had realized. But the more I learned about it, the more I wanted to do it.

But would we pass the test?

At the end of the interview, Gillian shook hands with everybody, even Emily Michelle. "I can see a guide dog puppy will get lots of good experience living with your family," she said to Watson.

"Does that mean we get the job?" Watson asked with a slow smile.

Gillian nodded. "I think you do."

"Hooray!" David Michael shouted, which made Shannon bark.

"When do we get the puppy?" Karen asked eagerly.

Gillian's answer took me by surprise. "We have a puppy ready right now. The couple who was going to raise her moved unexpectedly to another country. So the puppy came back to us. She's just turned four months old and her name is Scout. You can come get her this Saturday morning."

This weekend! Good grief! That was soon!

In a matter of days, we were going to have a new puppy in the house.

The Guide Dog Foundation is in Smithtown, Long Island, in New York, not far from where Abby used to live. From the front we saw what looked like a small, neat, square building behind a low white fence. I don't know what I expected, but I liked how friendly it looked.

We saw six new Labrador retriever puppies in the glassed-in puppy nursery area. We also saw about a hundred dogs, black and yellow Labradors, golden retrievers, and a few Shiloh shepherds, which looked like German shepherds to me. Some were in training. Some were being boarded for their owners or puppy walker families.

All of them greeted us by barking loudly and wagging their tails.

Behind the foundation are dorms, where people stay when they come to get their guide dogs and learn how to work with them. I wondered if they could hear the barking in their dorms, and if they could tell the sound of one dog's bark from another.

26

The dogs' name plates were on their kennel-run doors, along with the names of their sponsors. I loved Scout's name, in part because the narrator of one of my favorite books, *To Kill a Mockingbird*, is named Scout.

I couldn't help but think, the moment I saw Scout, that she was extra-special. She was a beautiful chocolate-colored Labrador retriever. I fell in love with her instantly.

We went through a training session and saw a video about guide dogs and how to be a good puppy walker. Then Gillian gave us the foundation handbook with all the basic information on raising Scout. She went over it with us, patiently answering all our questions. Both Mom and Watson took careful notes.

Scout came with her own collar, special ID tags, and leash. We also got two bowls, a starter bag of the kind of dog food we were supposed to feed her, a crate for her to sleep in, and two Nylabones for her to chew. We were also given a yellow coat for her to wear that identified her as a guide dog puppy in training so that she could be taken everywhere (just as she would be when she became a working guide dog). Oh yes, we got her medical records too, and forms we were supposed to fill out in order to keep track of her progress for the Guide Dog Foundation, with which we would be in touch at least once a month.

After Watson filled out some more forms, we put Scout in her crate (which was basically a big cage) and put the crate in the car. Scout looked a little anxious, but mostly calm. Karen and David Michael sat on either side of her.

Karen petted the kennel. "Don't worry, Scout," she said. "We're going to do everything just right. You're going to have the best puppy walker family in the whole wide world."

I hoped she was right.

CHAPTER 4

Abby just *happened* to be jogging by when we got home with Scout. Claudia and Shannon weren't even subtle about it. The moment we pulled up to the house, they walked out Shannon's front door and across the street.

Although Scout was a calm puppy, she was still wiggly and adorable and irresistible. Claudia melted instantly, falling on her knees and saying, "Oh, you are so-o-o-o-o cute." Shannon, meanwhile, was also kneeling next to Scout, talking baby talk.

Abby sneezed and said in a slightly thickened voice, "So you're Scout. Hello, girl." (I'd naturally kept the BSC members posted on every detail).

Scout wriggled her body enthusiastically.

Mom smiled. "I'll go get Shannon," she said. She was referring to Shannon our puppy. It was time for Shannon and Scout to meet. Even though Scout wouldn't be able to play with

29

Shannon, it was important to make them comfortable around each other. Thanks to Shannon and Mallory, I'd read *many* books, including two by dog trainers at a monastery, the Monks of New Skete, which Shannon had lent me, plus another one supplied by Mallory, written by a dog trainer named Carol Lea Benjamin, who was also a children's book writer. In all the books we'd read, we'd been told that this was the best way for a dog to meet a new dog coming into its house — on neutral territory.

According to the books, dogs are pack animals and every one of them behaves according to certain universal rules. The families the dogs live with become their packs. Just like in a real pack, dogs don't want newcomers in their packs without their permission.

Shannon came bounding out of the house and stopped when she saw Scout. Shannon's ears went up. Then she moved toward Scout. Shannon's tail was wagging a little (which is sometimes a sign of being uncertain about how to react to a situation, according to the dog books).

The moment Shannon got close to Scout, Scout said, "You're the boss! I'm friendly! Don't hurt me!"

How did she say that? In dog language, of course. Dogs use a lot of body language. Dog language for "You're the boss" is this: Scout rolled over on her back and put her paws in the air. Shannon sniffed Scout all over. Then she backed up slightly, put her front paws out in front of her in a dog bow, and said, "Woof!"

That's dog language for "Let's play!"

In an instant, Scout had rolled over, leaped up, and accepted the invitation. We let them spend time together for a few minutes and then we took them into the house.

"When do you start training her?" Abby asked.

"Right away," I said.

Claudia looked doubtful. "Isn't that awfully young? I mean, if puppies are like really little kids, they have about a two-second attention span."

"You're right about that, Claudia," Watson agreed. "We won't start out trying to teach her anything except how to be house-trained and how to get used to a leash and collar."

"But we're going to take her to puppy obedience classes right away," I said. "It helps her to get used to other dogs and new situations and teaches us how to start training her."

"Special classes for guide dogs?" Shannon asked. She was on the floor, scratching Scout's soft ears.

"They have classes we can go to at the foundation," I said. "But it's a long drive, so we'll probably go around here. We're only supposed to teach Scout basic obedience commands like 'sit' and 'stay.' You know, good manners for dogs. She'll learn the special guide dog stuff when she goes back to the foundation."

"This is *so* cool," said Abby. Then she sneezed again and added hastily, "Well, nice to meet you, Scout. I'd better get going."

"I can tell Scout's really smart," Claudia said.

"How?" I asked, secretly pleased.

"I just can," said Claudia loftily. "Artists have their ways. Oh, wow. I just had a terrific idea. Scout would make a great subject for an art piece."

"Would you like that, girl?" Shannon crooned. And Scout, since she was a very smart puppy, naturally wagged her tail, which this time didn't mean she was uncertain, I knew. It meant "Yes!"

Claudia was right about Scout being smart. I saw it was true the very next morning when I stumbled out onto the pavement, yawning. "Get busy," I said sleepily to Scout.

And you know what? She did, right away!

"This meeting of the BSC will now come to order," I announced. "No, Scout."

Scout was chewing on the leg of my chair.

"It's okay," said Claudia. "It's an old chair."

"She can't learn bad habits." Gently I pulled

Scout away from the chair leg and offered her the Nylabone I had brought. Nylabones are special bones that don't splinter or break off.

Without missing a chomp, Scout settled down with the Nylabone. Didn't I say she was smart?

Stacey looked at Abby and said, "Is this going to be okay, Abby? I mean, I know you're allergic to dogs."

"Omigosh," I said. I'd totally forgotten.

Abby just grinned. "I'm sitting next to an open window, it's only for half an hour, and if it gets too bad, I'll go outside. But I think it will be okay."

Relieved, I leaned back.

Claudia eyed Scout and said, "Does she always have to wear that little yellow coat?"

I nodded. "It identifies her. Later she'll learn to wear a special harness for guiding blind people. Right now we have to get her used to going different places, since she'll have to go anywhere her owner goes."

"Like McDonald's?" Claudia asked.

"Or the ballet?" Jessi asked.

"Everywhere," I said. "The law says a guide dog can go anywhere a person can go."

"And she has to learn to go to all those places and behave, right?" Mallory put in.

"Right," I said.

Just then the phone rang. Claudia picked it up and answered, "Baby-sitters Club." She listened for a moment and said, "One second, please."

Claud put her hand over the receiver, turned to us, and said, "It's the Coopers. I mean, it's Mrs. Cooper. She wanted to confirm the sitting job for tomorrow."

Mary Anne flipped open the record book. "I'll be there after school," she said.

Claudia told her Mary Anne would be there.

After Claudia had hung up, Abby said, "Shannon told Anna that Deb won't talk to anybody. Her friends at school have tried to call her and to visit her, and she won't talk to them."

"You can't blame her," said Jessi. "It all happened so quickly. She must still be in shock."

In a soft voice, Mary Anne said, "I'd want to talk to my friends."

"Sometimes if you have a problem, like when I first found out I had diabetes," Stacey volunteered, "and you think maybe people are treating you differently because they feel sorry for you, it makes you, well, uncomfortable."

Abby said, "It wouldn't make me uncomfortable. It would make me really angry. I never want anyone to treat me differently because of my asthma or my allergies."

Our eyes met for a moment and then we

both sort of smiled. Abby and I had had some problems when she'd first joined the BSC for that very reason. I had been worried that her asthma and allergies would interfere with her being an effective baby-sitter.

Boy, had she ever proved me wrong!

Mary Anne didn't say anything. She folded her hands tightly together, and I could tell she was upset.

Quickly I said, "Don't worry, Mary Anne. You're not baby-sitting for Deb, just her brothers. It'll be okay."

But Mary Anne shook her head. "I'm not worried about that," she said. "I just wish I could make Deb feel better. I wish there was something I could *do*."

Then she leaned forward and pressed her cheek against the top of Scout's head. Scout stopped chewing her bone long enough to tip her muzzle back and give Mary Anne's chin a quick lick.

"Good girl," I heard Mary Anne murmur. "Good girl."

CHAPTER 5

Tuesday

When I went to the Coopers', I didn't know I was even going to see Deb. The truth is, I wasn't sure I wanted to see her. I was almost afraid to. I didn't know what I would say. But nothing I said would have mattered to Deb anyway.

Mark Cooper is eight and Jed is four, and they are outgoing kids, full of energy and ready for anything. Mark has dark curly hair and glasses and is a sturdy kid who is fond of sports and comic books. Jed, with lighter brown hair, also curly, has a recently developed fascination with puzzles and dinosaurs.

Since the day was gray and drizzly, Mary Anne wasn't surprised to find Jed on the floor with the pieces of a giant dinosaur puzzle spread out around him. He was holding one piece in his hand.

"Don't tell me!" he commanded as Mary Anne walked into the family room, where Mrs. Cooper had sent her after answering the door. She'd conferred with Mary Anne briefly, then hurried away, looking harried.

Jed leaned forward and pressed the piece into place. "See? I *knew* where it was supposed to go."

Mark, who was sprawled on the sofa with a comic book, shook his head. "I don't think so," he said. "I think you got lucky."

"When you get eaten by a dinosaur," said Jed placidly, "you'll be sorry."

"Hi, guys," Mary Anne interrupted. From the hall, she heard Mrs. Cooper say, "Deb, please."

"Is *she* down there?" Mary Anne heard Deb say.

"Mary Anne? Yes. I told you, she's sitting for Mark and Jed."

"Close the door," Deb demanded.

Mrs. Cooper appeared in the doorway, glanced into the family room, and saw that Mary Anne had heard. She smiled. "Don't forget your homework, Mark. Mary Anne, we'll be back very soon," Mrs. Cooper said brightly, closing the door between the hall and the family room. A minute later, Mary Anne heard two sets of footsteps: Mrs. Cooper's heavier tread and another pair of feet making slow, uncertain steps, like a child learning to walk.

Then the back door opened and closed, and they were gone.

Mary Anne felt her throat tighten. She knew the second set of footsteps had belonged to Deb, who was trying to negotiate a familiar hall made unfamiliar by darkness.

Glancing over at the two boys, Mary Anne wondered if they were ignoring what had just happened, or if it really hadn't made an impression on them. Jed was intently studying another puzzle piece featuring the toothy grin of a T-rex. Mark was staring down at his comic book with equal intensity.

Taking a deep breath, Mary Anne said, "Your

mother mentioned something about home-work, Mark."

Mark rolled his eyes. "I'm too young to have homework."

"*Mark,*" Mary Anne insisted, hiding a smile.

"Oh, all right. I'm supposed to read another chapter of *Nate the Great.*"

"I know that book," Mary Anne offered. "It's a good one. You want to read it aloud to me?"

"Me too," Jed chimed in. "Read to me too."

"How does that sound, Mark?" Mary Anne asked.

Mark shrugged. "Okay."

Of course, they couldn't start reading right away. Mark had to explain what the book was about to Jed. Then Jed said that *he* had a book he wanted to read. Then Mark claimed that he should go first, which of course made Jed protest.

"We'll have plenty of time to read from both books," Mary Anne promised. "But we'll start with Mark, because he has to do this for school. Okay, Jed? Then we'll take a break and make some popcorn and read your book."

Jed thought for a minute. Then he nodded and climbed up next to Mary Anne on the sofa. He gave Mark a look and said, "Come on, Mark. So we can have popcorn."

But when Mark finished the chapter, Jed had

changed his mind. "Read more," he pleaded.

"You want to read another chapter?" Mary Anne asked Mark.

Mark looked pleased. "Okay," he said.

When he had finished the second chapter, Mark crowed triumphantly, "Ha, I'm ahead of everybody."

"My turn now," Jed announced. "Then we can have popcorn."

They had just finished reading Jed's book when the back door opened and Mrs. Cooper called, "We're home."

Mary Anne got up and followed Jed and Mark into the kitchen. Mrs. Cooper and Deb were standing there. Deb was motionless except for her head, which she turned from side to side. She was wearing dark glasses, and she seemed to be scrunched up inside her clothes, as if she wanted to hide in them.

"Hi, guys," Mrs. Cooper said, ruffling Jed's hair. "Can you believe it? Dr. Whitehurst saw us right away."

"Having a blind person in her waiting room is bad for business, that's why," Deb spat.

"Now, Deb," said her mother while Mary Anne tried not to look shocked. "You don't mean that." She patted her daughter's arm.

"Don't I?" Deb jerked her arm away.

Mrs. Cooper glanced at Mary Anne and said, "I need to run across the street and feed our neighbors' cats, water their plants, and bring in their mail and newspapers — they're on vacation. Could I leave Deb here with you?"

"Sure," Mary Anne answered. "We were about to make some popcorn if that's okay."

"*Popcorn*," Deb repeated in a scornful voice.

"How about some fruit and cookies or crackers? You like those," Mrs. Cooper asked her. She caught Deb by the elbow. "Why don't you sit here at the table, sweetie, and —"

Again, Deb jerked her arm free of her mother. "I can find my way to the table," she snapped. "And I don't need a baby-sitter!"

Walking away from Mrs. Cooper, Deb bumped into a chair at the table. The chair fell. Deb groped as if she were trying to stop it, but when her hands met the edge of the table, she held on. Mary Anne saw that her knuckles were white.

Mark quickly picked up the chair. "Here, Deb," he said. "The chair is right in front of you."

Without speaking, Deb reached out with one hand, found the chair, and lowered herself carefully into the seat. Then, still gripping the table edge, she scooted the chair up to it.

"I'll be right back," Mrs. Cooper assured Mary Anne and hurried out the kitchen door.

For a moment, everyone was silent. Then Deb turned in Mary Anne's general direction and said, "What's the matter, Mary Anne? Haven't you ever seen a blind person before?"

"No," Mary Anne replied, before she could think. Then she turned bright red.

Jed said suddenly, "I'll go pick up my puzzle! I'll be right back."

He sounded so stricken with guilt that Mary Anne told him, "Jed, it's okay. You haven't finished it yet."

"No, it's not okay," Jed insisted. "We have to pick things up and we can't move things around because Deb can't see them anymore and she might fall."

Then he disappeared down the hall.

Deb said in a harsh voice, "My clothes are organized by color now. That's so I don't wear things that don't match. I'm supposed to know what colors are in what drawers. How'd I do? Am I wearing something gross?"

"You look nice," Mary Anne said.

"Ha," Deb replied.

Mary Anne took a deep breath. She went to the refrigerator and said, "Let's see — there are grapes and oranges in the refrigerator. And where's the popcorn?"

"We have graham crackers," Mark said. "I like graham crackers. We don't need popcorn." Mary Anne saw him sneak a look at his sister, then look away.

"Okay. That sounds like a pretty good snack," Mary Anne said. She got out the grapes, washed them, and put them in a bowl. She handed Mark a plate so he could spread the graham crackers on it. Then she cut an orange into sections and put them on a plate on the table. By that time, Jed had returned.

Mark put an orange slice, some graham crackers, and some grapes on a plate and pushed it toward his sister. "Here, Deb," he offered. "Your snack is right in front of you."

"I'm not hungry," she stated flatly. Then she said to Mary Anne, "Mary Anne, *do* I look different?"

Mary Anne looked at Deb. She was an older version of Mark, an athletic girl with short dark hair. But in contrast to Mark's ruddy complexion, Deb was pale and thinner than Mary Anne remembered her to be. Her dark glasses unnerved Mary Anne.

"I don't know," Mary Anne answered carefully. "Do you have to wear — I mean — the sunglasses?"

Ignoring the question, Deb said, "It doesn't matter what I look like. It's not my problem. I don't have to look at me. I can't see me. I can't see *anything*." She began to laugh.

Where was Mrs. Cooper? Mary Anne glanced toward the door and then said desperately, trying to stop the edgy laughter that was coming from Deb, "Have a cracker, Deb. Don't you at least want a cracker?"

Deb pushed back from the table. "Polly doesn't want a cracker!" She stood up and the chair went over again with a crash. "I don't need a cracker. I don't need a baby-sitter. I can take care of myself. I can, I can, I can."

Mrs. Cooper came rushing through the back door as Deb's voice rose. "Deb, dear," she said in an anguished tone.

"Leave me alone!" Deb screamed. "You don't know what it's like. You don't know. One minute you can see and the next minute you're blind. I can't even remember the last thing I saw before I — I — "

Deb threw her hands out. The table rocked. Juice spilled and grapes rolled from the plate. Her mother put her arms around Deb as Deb began to cry hot, angry tears.

Mary Anne immediately began trying to clean up the mess, hardly knowing what she was doing.

"That's okay," Mrs. Cooper told her. "Just leave it. And thanks, Mary Anne. I'll take care of everything now."

Mary Anne jumped up. "Okay," she replied. She said good-bye to Mark and Jed and left as quickly as she could.

Mary Anne left in a hurry partly because she

44

didn't know how to react to what had just happened, but also because the lump had come back into her throat and she was afraid she might start to cry herself.

Deb was as angry as anyone Mary Anne had ever seen, and Mary Anne's heart broke for her.

But nothing she could think of to say or do would be any help. Mary Anne knew the only person who could help Deb now was Deb. And Mary Anne suspected that Deb was much too angry to even begin to try.

CHAPTER 6

Did I mention how smart Scout was? She was totally, totally brilliant. She'd already more or less figured out house-training when we got her. She hardly ever made a mistake. The more we trained her, the calmer she seemed.

Not that she didn't break into puppy wiggles and tail-wagging marathons whenever she met *anyone*. To Scout, everyone in the whole world was a potential best friend. And of course, most people fell in love with her the moment they saw her.

But we still couldn't let her jump up on people to say hello. She had to sit politely before we would let one of her admirers pet her.

You'd be amazed at the number of people who said, "Oh, it's okay," when Scout jumped up. But I kept explaining that it *wasn't* okay, since Scout was in training for a very important job (just in case they hadn't noticed her beautiful guide-dog-in-training jacket).

I quickly learned to answer all kinds of questions. One person even asked me if Scout was blind! I explained that she wasn't, but that someday she'd act as the "eyes" for a blind person.

As soon as we got Scout, we started taking her everywhere. When Watson went into his office, he took Scout. Mom took her to work too. Nannie took her to her bowling league and to her garden club meetings.

And of course I took her to BSC meetings.

The second time I took her, I was sure to get there early. Claudia immediately said, "Oh, I guess I'd better put the snacks away."

"Nope. Pass them around," I ordered. "Scout has to learn not to beg."

"It seems so mean," Claudia said. But from the way her hand was clutching the bag of Cheez Doodles, I knew that I wouldn't have to work too hard to persuade her to keep the junk food out and available.

I clinched it by saying, "Besides, if it were chocolate, you couldn't give Scout a piece anyway. Chocolate is really bad for dogs and can even kill some of them."

"Oh, right," said Claudia. She put the Cheez Doodles on her desk and bent down to scratch Scout behind her ears. Scout immediately began to wriggle. We both laughed. Scout had held her sitting position — but only by wagging practically her entire body.

Abby came in and said, "Twist and shout, it's little Scout!"

"You're starting to sound like Vanessa," said Mal, who followed Abby into Claudia's room. Vanessa is Mal's next-youngest sister and wants to be a poet, something she practices at every spoken or written opportunity.

"Thanks, Mal. You're a pal," Abby replied.

We groaned. Then Jessi came in with Mary Anne and Stacey, and I pronounced, "This meeting of the Baby-sitters Club will come to order."

We spent the rest of the meeting rubbing Scout's stomach and talking baby talk to her. I figured it was good baby-sitting practice.

In the middle of our Scout-admiration session, Mr. Cooper called. He needed someone to stay with Deb the following Thursday afternoon.

I told him I'd call him back and hung up the phone. Mary Anne paused before she flipped open the record book. We'd all heard about her encounter with Deb and knew that staying with her wouldn't be an easy job.

Mary Anne said, "I have the Hobarts that afternoon and Claudia has the Kuhns. Jessi has dance class and Mal has a dentist appointment. . . ."

"Thanks for reminding me," muttered Mallory.

"And Stacey —"

"— has major homework," Stacey finished for her.

Mary Anne nodded and made a note in the record book. Then she said, "That leaves you, Kristy. Maybe you'll have better luck with Deb than I did."

"Maybe," I said. "It helps to know what to expect."

Mary Anne nodded, but I thought she looked doubtful. I admit, I felt a pang of worry too. But I didn't let it show as I called Mr. Cooper back to confirm the job.

He said, "Oh, good, Kristy. And it's not really baby-sitting, you know. That's what we told Deb. She insists that she can handle being on her own, but we told her we just want someone around in case of an emergency."

"No problem," I said, but with a lot more assurance than I felt.

After I hung up, we talked a little more about Mary Anne's sitting session at the Coopers'. I still hadn't seen Deb. In fact, as we talked, we realized that Mary Anne was the only person we knew who had seen Deb since she'd lost her eyesight.

That surprised me. I knew from Shannon that Deb probably wasn't planning to go back

49

to school, since the school year would be ending by the time she was ready to go full-time. I had assumed that Deb still didn't feel like dealing with other people. But she was going to have to, sooner or later, even if she didn't go back to school right away. It wasn't going to get any easier if she waited.

That was when I had my brilliant idea. "Listen," I told Mary Anne and Claudia. "What do you think about bringing the Hobarts and Kuhns by to visit when I stay with Deb? You know, just drop by, get her used to the idea of other people. Since they're not classmates of hers, it might be easier."

Mary Anne said, "I don't know. . . ."

"It might work," Mallory decided. "She can't say no if you just show up."

"It seems to me she's been through enough shocks lately," Stacey argued. "What if it's too much?"

"Well, we can just leave," Claudia said.

We thought about it a moment and then, to my surprise, Mary Anne said, "Well, maybe it's worth a try. Claudia's right. We can always leave if it's too much."

With Mary Anne's seal of approval, how could we miss?

"Done deal," I concluded.

We fielded a few more calls and then it was time to go. Charlie was waiting at the curb when Abby, Scout, and I came out. "We have to go to the grocery store on the way home," he said. "Watson gave me a list."

"Cool," I said. "Scout hasn't been to the grocery store yet. Have you, Scout?"

Hearing her name, Scout pricked up her ears and thumped her tail. At the grocery store, Scout walked on her leash like the perfect puppy she was, hardly pulling at all. We talked to two people who were also grocery shopping, and I told them about Scout and the Guide Dog Foundation. One of the people, a young woman, took down the address of the foundation, declaring that she was going to make a donation. The other person, an older man, told us that we were "proof that the younger generation isn't as bad as everyone says," and congratulated us.

I guess that's what made what happened next so surprising. We'd just turned down the cereal aisle when a thin woman said in a loud voice, "Well, I never!"

The woman stared hard at us and then pointed at Scout. "What is that animal doing in here?" she demanded even more loudly.

"This is Scout," I said proudly. "She's a guide dog in training."

"I don't care. Dogs are not allowed in the grocery store. Didn't you read the sign?" Now the woman's voice was not only loud but getting shrill. Scout sat down and stared up at the woman.

"As a guide dog in training, Scout has permission to be in the store," Abby insisted politely.

"To make messes. And what if someone is allergic?"

"I'm allergic," Abby replied, and I could tell she was about to ignite. "What Scout is doing is a lot more important than my allergies."

"I don't appreciate your tone," said the woman.

"Well, you can check with the manager," said Abby, kind of rudely.

"I will!" the woman exclaimed angrily. She marched past us, pushing her shopping cart as if it were a battering ram.

I looked around. Charlie had inconveniently disappeared.

We didn't see the woman again until we were headed for the checkout counter. This time, she was dragging a man in shirtsleeves and tie beside her. "There they are!" she said. I half expected her to add, "Arrest them!"

But she didn't. She just stood, a picture of outrage, pointing at Scout as if Scout were a plague dog or something.

The manager's name tag read "Tom Feldman." He was young and he had friendly brown eyes. I said, "Hi, Mr. Feldman."

"What seems to be the problem here?" he asked.

"This is Scout," I explained. "She's a guide dog in training." I pointed to her jacket.

Mr. Feldman squatted down beside Scout. I thought she might jump up, but she didn't. She wagged her tail and managed to swipe the tip of his chin with her tongue.

"Disgusting," I heard the woman say. "Unsanitary."

Mr. Feldman stood up. "She seems fine," he said. "I assume she's house-trained — or store-trained."

"Yes," I said.

"Aren't you going to throw them out of the store?" the woman insisted, her voice growing even louder. Scout's ears pricked up.

Several people at the checkout had stopped to stare. I was embarrassed but also angry.

Then, to my amazement, Mr. Feldman said, "Guide dogs in training, just like guide dogs and all other service dogs, are welcome in this store."

My mouth dropped open.

Abby's mouth dropped open.

The woman's mouth dropped open. Then she said, "Well! I'm taking my business elsewhere."

Mr. Feldman nodded. "I'm sorry you feel that way," he said.

The woman left her full cart right there and turned and stomped out of the store.

Three people in the next checkout line applauded!

Abby whooped.

Mr. Feldman's face turned bright, bright red. "See you again soon, Scout," he said and hurried away.

Charlie came out of the far aisle with an armful of groceries and dumped them into our cart.

"I thought I heard someone yelling," he said with feigned innocence. "Did I miss anything?"

Abby and I looked at each other and burst out laughing.

CHAPTER 7

Deb was sitting in the family room when Mr. Cooper escorted me in. The shades were drawn. The lights were off. It was downright gloomy.

"Wow," I blurted out. "It's dark in here."

Deb turned her head toward the sound of my voice. "No kidding," she said sarcastically.

Mr. Cooper patted me on the shoulder as I began to stammer out an apology. "It *is* dark in here," he said. He opened the blinds and turned on a lamp.

"You remember Kristy, Deb," Mr. Cooper said in a conversational tone of voice. "Mom works with her dad."

Deb didn't answer.

"Mrs. Cooper will be home from work at six o'clock," Mr. Cooper went on after a pause. "The boys and I should be back by then. There's a number on the table by the phone in the kitchen where you can reach us if there's an emergency."

"Don't worry, Dad," Deb said bitterly. "I won't move until you get back. I wouldn't want to cause the *baby-sitter* any trouble."

She spoke with such venom that I was taken aback.

"Deborah," Mr. Cooper cautioned. Then he sighed quietly and shook his head. He patted my shoulder and left without another word.

Suddenly my brilliant idea didn't seem so brilliant. I wished I had thought about it a little longer.

I said, "Uh, Deb?" Should I warn her? Prepare her for her unexpected and probably unwelcome visitors?

"That's my name," Deb shot back, staring at nothing. Then she said, "It's called angle closure glaucoma. That's the disease I have. It's hereditary — my grandmother had it — but it could happen to anyone."

I swallowed hard.

"It could happen to you," she said. "Right now."

I blinked. I was at a loss for words, a totally unfamiliar feeling.

Deb went on. "I had a bad headache. It went on for a few days. Then I started seeing these, like, halos around lights and things." She

56

laughed bitterly. "I didn't tell anyone because I didn't want to get glasses."

"Mal has glasses," I said. "So do Mary Anne and Abby. So does my little sister Karen."

Deb ignored my stupid comment. She continued, "Then I woke up one morning and I was sick. I threw up and I threw up again and then I couldn't see. They took me to the hospital but it was too late. Even surgery didn't help."

Watson had talked a little about what had happened to Deb, but it wasn't the same as hearing it from her — hearing her words drop, hard and ugly, into the silence of the family room.

"So that's it," she went on. "Now I'm the town blind girl. Are there people at the windows looking in? You could charge them a quarter apiece and make some money."

"Stop it!" I cried, horrified at what she was saying. She didn't sound like a twelve-year-old at all. She sounded like a bitter adult.

"You're staring at me," she said.

I was. But I was staring now because I was so shocked by her words. "Because I don't know what to say to you," I blurted out.

Deb said softly, "I wish you did."

It was just at that moment that the front doorbell rang.

Deb's head jerked around. "Who's that?" She pushed up from her chair.

"I'll get it," I said quickly.

Mary Anne stood at the door with the two oldest Hobart boys — Ben, who is eleven, and James, who is eight.

"Where are Jed and Mark?" James asked.

"They have a doctor's appointment," I told him.

"Better them than us, mate," said Ben with a cheeky grin. (The Hobarts are from Australia.)

"We're on our way to the park. Want to come?" James asked. He waved his baseball glove in the air enticingly.

At that moment, Claudia called, "Mary Anne, Kristy, hey, you guys!"

James Hobart saw Jake Kuhn, who is the same age he is, and said instantly, "You can be on my team."

Laurel Kuhn, who is six, was holding a soccer ball. She said, "But I want to play soccer, not baseball."

"Football's good too," said Ben.

Laurel looked puzzled for a moment, then said, "Oh, that's what people in Australia call soccer."

"No," Ben replied. "Soccer is what people in the United States call football."

Patsy Kuhn, who is five, didn't say anything.

She held on to Claudia's hand and looked thoughtful.

"What's happening, Kristy?" Claudia asked. "We're on our way to the park. Want to come?"

If I hadn't known it was all planned, I wouldn't have known. Claudia and Mary Anne sounded completely believable. But I still didn't think Deb was going to be too happy at their arrival.

"Uh," I said, at a loss for words for the second time in one afternoon.

"Is Mark home?" asked Jake, peering past me. "He can be on my team too. And you can be the umpire, Kristy, since you know about baseball."

"Mark and Jed aren't here," Ben said.

"What about Deb?" Claudia asked. "Is she around? Maybe we could say hello."

I shook my head at Claudia, but she didn't notice.

The mention of Deb's name brought on an immediate silence. I could tell that no one knew quite what to say. Then Mary Anne said, "Maybe Deb would like to walk to the park with us."

"I don't know," I said, trying to stall for time.

"Why don't you ask her?" Ben inquired.

What could I do? I turned and went back down the hall to the family room. Before I realized what was happening, everyone else followed. When I stopped at the door of the family room, they all stopped too.

Deb jerked around. "Who's there?" she said. "Who is it?"

"It's me. Kristy," I said. "And . . ."

"Hi, Deb," said Ben. "It's Ben Hobart. And James. We're on our way to the park with Mary Anne and we thought you might like to come along."

"We're going too," Patsy chimed in.

As each person spoke, Deb's head jerked toward the sound. Then she seemed to shrink into the chair as if she wanted to disappear.

After a long moment of waiting for Deb to speak, Jake said, "We're going to play baseball. Or maybe soccer."

"Football," Laurel insisted, grinning at Ben.

Deb spoke then. "I'll make a deal," she said sarcastically. "I'll come play with you if everyone wears a blindfold. That'll make it even."

I saw Claudia's eyes widen, and I heard Ben mutter, "Whoa."

I felt myself getting angry. I knew Deb was hurting, but it seemed so unfair for her to take it out on little kids. I said, as evenly as I could manage, "Well, you don't have to go to the park, Deb."

"We'd better be going," Claudia said at the same time.

"Yup," Jake agreed. I noticed that he wasn't quite looking at Deb. In fact, he was looking everywhere but at her. Patsy, however, had released Claudia's hand and stepped into the room. She walked up close to Deb, staring. Then she held up her hand and waved it.

Of course Deb couldn't see her. "Oh," said Patsy. "You really can't see me!"

Deb jumped a little when she heard how near Patsy was to her. Then she said, "Who's there? Who are you?"

"Patsy, Patsy Kuhn. I'm five."

By this time, Claudia had reached Patsy. She caught her by the hand and said, "We should be going, Patsy."

Jake said, "If you can't see, does that mean you have to stay in this room? I mean, can't you walk around or anything?"

Deb said, "I could if I wanted to. But I don't want to. I like it here."

"It's a nice day out," Laurel said softly.

"Well, I'm blind and I can't see it. So why don't you just go and play and leave me alone."

Patsy looked back over her shoulder. She said, "I'm sorry."

"Don't be sorry for me," Deb replied icily. "Don't you *dare* be sorry for me. I don't need your pity. You don't have to visit me and be nice to me. In fact, the nicest thing you could do is just leave me alone!"

Claudia and Mary Anne quickly herded the Kuhns and the Hobarts out of the doorway. (They didn't need much convincing.)

"I'll go let people out," I said to Deb, so she wouldn't continue talking to an empty room.

"Do that." The rage in Deb's voice made me wince. "And tell them that it was nice to *see* them."

I caught up with everyone at the front door.

"I guess my brilliant idea wasn't so brilliant after all," I said.

"I guess not," said Claudia.

James asked, "She doesn't really have to stay in the house, does she?"

"No," Mary Anne told him. "She's just not ready to come out yet, that's all."

"It'd be hard," Ben said. He shook his head. "Awfully hard."

"We'd better get to the park," Claudia said. "See you later, Kristy."

"See ya," I said. I closed the door and went back to join Deb, with a heavy heart. When I reached the family room, I discovered that Deb had turned on the television.

"Deb," I began.

She picked up the remote and after a few seconds of fumbling, cranked up the volume. "That's a hint," she said. "Leave me alone."

So I sat silently with Deb Cooper until her mother came home.

CHAPTER 8

What a beautiful day, I thought, stretching and yawning. Then I remembered it was Saturday and decided it was an even more beautiful day. I got up, got dressed, and went downstairs to eat a Breakfast of Coaches and Champions.

Wise coach that I am, I had foreseen it was going to be a beautiful day and had called a Krushers' practice for that morning.

The Krushers, as you may remember, is the kids' softball team I coach, with Abby as my assistant coach. It's mostly for really little kids. Some kids who are older and on other teams also play on the team, but the average age of the approximately twenty regular players is 5.8. Our full name is Kristy's Krushers, which was the name given us by Jackie Rodowsky, a good ball player and terrific sport who has the amazing ability to get into all kinds of weird and sometimes funny accidents wherever he goes.

David Michael and Karen were ready and waiting at the kitchen table. Their gloves were by their plates, and although we didn't have a game that day, Karen was wearing her Krushers shirt. She's the only one on the team who spells it with a "C." Karen is a stickler for accuracy.

"Hi, Krushers," I said, making myself a cereal combo. Cereal combos are one of the nice things about having lots of different people in a family. It means that you aren't usually stuck with one variety of cereal. I passed on Watson's low-fat cereal with extra bran, and went instead for a combo of Rice Krispies (Nannie's favorite), plain cornflakes (Charlie's), and granola mix (Mom's).

"Can we take Scout to practice?" Karen asked.

"I don't see why not, if Watson says it's okay," I answered.

"Shannon too," David Michael insisted.

Watson, who'd been reading his newspaper at the end of the table with Scout at his side, looked up. "Daddy, please?" Karen begged, clasping her hands together dramatically, as if she were pleading for someone's life.

I saw Watson's lips twitch. "We-e-ell," he said.

"Pleeeeease," Karen repeated.

"Okay," Watson decided, which was a signal

for Karen to take off like a shot to get Scout's leash and yellow jacket, with David Michael right behind her to get Shannon's gear.

We ambled to practice, giving Shannon and Scout time to thoroughly sniff everything that interested them. Since Shannon was older than Scout, she was more used to being on a leash, and I think it helped Scout to see Shannon taking everything in stride.

Even though it was early, the school playground was already getting crowded. Fortunately, the softball diamond hadn't been claimed by anyone yet, except for a lone jogger methodically rounding the bases.

Abby. Of course. She's as competitive as I am, if not more so. I should have known that she would be here even earlier, to make sure no one else took "our" field.

I waved to her. She waved back and jogged to me.

As everyone arrived, Shannon got her usual share of attention, and naturally Scout got a good bit of attention too. Shannon demonstrated her newest trick, holding out her paw on the command of "shake." I heard Karen explaining importantly to James Hobart that Scout was still a very young puppy and didn't know that trick yet. "But when she grows up, she's going to be trained to be a real, live guide dog," Karen told him and the surrounding audience. "She'll be able to help a blind person go anywhere. To school. On planes. On *safaris*."

I blew the whistle and called the practice to order. Karen and David Michael left Scout and Shannon inside the dugout fence in the shade and walked out onto the field.

We practiced baserunning, which sounds really basic, and should be. But on a team with players of so many ages, it's not as easy as it sounds. Very young players, such as five-year-old Claire Pike, Mal's youngest sister, can hit the ball if you throw it right at the bat. But often, when young players do connect with the ball, they are so thrilled to get a hit they stand there beaming with pride and forget to run at all.

Claire remembered to run this time and to stop at first base. But when she ran to second, she kept on going before she realized that third base wasn't somewhere in the outfield.

She skidded to a stop and came back to second with a sheepish look on her face. I half expected her to throw a temper tantrum (a Claire specialty), but instead she just said, "Am I out?"

"No," I assured her. "In a real game you would be, because a runner has to stay inside the baseline. But this is practice, so we can keep doing it until you get it right."

We did the play over. This time, Claire stopped at second.

Jake Kuhn, who is not a natural athlete and prefers soccer to softball, surprised us by getting a double.

Then Jackie slid into third base and somehow managed to peel the sole off his left cleat.

He stuck his foot in the air and said, "Wow, look!" as if he'd done something remarkable.

In a way, I guess he had. I'd never seen anything like that happen before.

Naturally the whole team headed toward Jackie to see what had happened. Abby and I exchanged a glance and then Abby said, "Water break!"

The Krushers were giggling and laughing as Jackie wiggled his toes in the air from the bottom of his shoe, where the sole had been.

Abby looked at Jackie's foot thoughtfully and said, "I think it's time you got some new baseball shoes, Jackie. What do you think?"

Jackie grinned as I reached down to give him a hand. "Yeah. I guess."

"Do you have any other shoes here?" I asked him.

"My sneakers," Jackie replied. "I'll put them on."

"Good idea," I said and turned my attention to planning the next drill with Abby.

Which is why I didn't notice what Karen was doing.

I didn't discover it until the end of practice, when we went back to the dugout to find Scout happily chewing on what remained of Jackie's peeled cleat. Shannon had the other one.

"Scout! Shannon!" I shouted in an alarmed voice, leaping forward to rescue the cleats. Shannon gave me a guilty look. Scout looked surprised and a little inquisitive when I snatched the shoes from her jaws. "How did you get these shoes? No!"

"I gave the shoes to them," Karen said. Her cheeks were bright red. "Jackie couldn't wear them anymore anyway and the puppies looked bored."

"You should never, *ever* give shoes to any dog to chew," I said, much more emphatically than I probably needed to. "How is a dog supposed to know which shoes she can chew and which shoes she can't?"

"Oh," Karen mumbled. "I never thought about that."

"Well, you have to think, Karen," I said. "Unless you want to ruin Scout's chances of ever becoming a guide dog."

"I'm sorry," Karen cried, her face growing even redder.

Abby intervened. "That's okay. I'm sure that

just this once no harm was done — except to what was left of Jackie's shoes." Her light tone seemed to reassure Karen.

I felt like a jerk. Had I overreacted or what? "Sorry, Karen," I apologized.

Karen looked at me and then at Abby and crossed her heart. "I promise, I won't give them any more shoes," she assured us. "Never, ever, ever."

I told Watson when we got home what had happened. I wasn't telling on Karen. I was just making sure that Scout's chances for becoming a guide dog weren't ruined.

Watson didn't seem too bothered. "It was a mistake," he said. "And if it doesn't happen again, I don't think any harm was done. If you'd like, I'll ask Gillian the next time I talk to her."

"Thanks," I said. "Wow, this is harder than I thought. I mean, you never know if one little thing is going to affect a puppy for her whole life." I turned to go to my room, then stopped and turned back as a thought hit me.

"Watson?"

"Yes, Kristy."

"It's kind of like raising children, isn't it? I mean, trying to get it right and worrying that something you do will affect them forever. . . ." My voice trailed off. Would Watson think it was some kind of insult, comparing raising dogs to raising children?

But Watson was smiling. "There *are* similarities, Kristy. But I will say this — puppies are a lot easier to potty train."

I burst out laughing then. "Thanks, Watson," I said. "Thanks a lot."

CHAPTER 9

Monday
 Mark and Jed don't quite know
what to do about Deb. They feel for
her, but I think they're afraid of
her too. And I think they're afraid
that they could go blind just like
she did . . . .

When Stacey arrived at the Coopers' for her baby-sitting job, she noticed that Deb was already sitting in the car, facing straight ahead.

"Hi, Deb," Stacey said. "It's me. Stacey."

"Hello," Deb replied expressionlessly. She didn't move.

Stacey saw that Mrs. Cooper was standing at the front door, holding it open. "I'm not late, am I?" Stacey said, checking her watch.

"Right on time," Mrs. Cooper assured her. "Deb just wanted to go out to the car a little early."

"Oh," said Stacey. Was it because Deb didn't want Stacey to see her being led to the car? Or did she just want to avoid Stacey altogether?

"Hi, Stacey," Mark greeted her from inside the doorway.

"Hello! *Good*-bye," shouted Jed, following his older brother into the hall. He began to giggle.

"Hi, guys." Stacey smiled back at them.

"We shouldn't be at the hospital for more than an hour, maybe an hour and a half," Mrs. Cooper told her. "I'll call you if it's going to take longer than that. We have an appointment with the social worker. I hope Deb will talk to her."

Stacey didn't know what to say to that, so she didn't say anything. Mrs. Cooper hugged

Mark and Jed and said, "See you in a little while." She paused, then added, "No television, okay?"

"Aw, Mom." Marked groaned.

Mrs. Cooper said, "Aw, Mark," and smiled as she left.

"What's a social worker?" Jed asked Stacey.

"Someone who helps people with problems," Stacey explained.

"I don't think it's fair," Mark said. "Deb doesn't have to go to school and she can watch whatever she wants on television. Well, listen to whatever she wants, anyway."

He suddenly looked guilt-stricken. He glanced down at his feet.

Jed, with the directness of a four-year-old, grabbed Stacey's arm and said, "What if I get sick like Deb and go blind too?"

Stacey thought quickly, then said, "Have you been to the doctor lately?"

"Yes. Last week." Mark made a face.

"Did the doctor say you were okay?"

"She said we were fine and she gave us a Charm pop," Jed said.

"Well, then, if the doctor said you're fine, then you're fine."

That seemed to reassure them, at least for the moment.

To change the subject, Stacey said, "Why don't we go outside and play?"

"Okay," Jed answered, taking off for the back door. By the time Stacey and Mark had followed, Jed was already banging around the yard like a pinball.

"We could have a water fight," Mark suggested hopefully, glancing toward the hose.

"It's still a little too chilly for that," Stacey replied.

"Baseball," Jed voted.

"How about kickball?" asked Stacey. She isn't good at sports, but she knew she could kick and catch a ball.

"Okay," Mark agreed. He found the kickball while Stacey and Jed set up a home plate and a base.

They did a few practice kicks first. Mark could kick the ball hard enough for Stacey to have to chase it a little bit, but Jed put more energy into giggling than into kicking. After a quick survey of the talent, Stacey appointed herself ball thrower. She made the rule that if she caught a ball that Jed kicked, she had to turn around twice while holding the ball before she could throw it at him to get him out.

"But just once for you, Mark. You're older."

"I know," Mark said. "Throw the ball."

Mark kicked the ball hard on the first try and made it to base. He put his hands on his knees and bent down low. "Come on, Jed, kick it hard!" he cried.

Stacey rolled the ball. Jed giggled, swung his foot wildly at it — and missed.

He fell down and laughed even harder. Mark snorted and began to laugh too. Stacey bent over to give Jed a hand. "You okay?" she asked.

Jed got up, laughing loudly. "I missed," he said.

"You sure did," Stacey agreed. "Strike one."

"How many strikes do I get?" Jed asked.

"Lots," Stacey told him. She rolled the ball again.

This time Jed made a good kick. The ball almost reached Stacey. She picked it up and spun around twice. When she finished spinning, Mark had just touched home plate. And Jed was standing there, watching all the action.

"Run!" Mark shouted. "Run, or you'll be out." He gave Jed a push.

"Oh!" Jed exclaimed and ran for the base.

Stacey threw the ball and missed (on purpose). Jed jumped with both feet onto the base, then stood and watched as Stacey ran after the ball. Stacey couldn't help but grin. She'd watched me coach softball before and was familiar with the "little kids forgetting to run" syndrome.

"Run home!" Mark bellowed at the top of his lungs. "Jed, run back to me!"

"Oh!" Jed passed third and ran home. He just barely beat Stacey, who had gotten a bad case of the giggles herself.

When she'd recovered, she looked up to see Mark and Jed watching her. "Why're you laughing?" Mark asked seriously. "We're winning."

Mark and Jed were beating Stacey a million to one (according to Jed) when Stacey rolled a ball to Mark and he closed his eyes before he kicked. He connected with it solidly. Then, with his eyes still closed, he ran toward where he thought the base would be.

He didn't touch the base. He crashed into Stacey as she was bending to catch the ball.

They both went down.

"Oof." Stacey gasped, caught by surprise.

Mark lay where he had fallen, with his eyes squeezed tightly shut.

"Mark? Mark, are you okay?" Stacey asked. She got to her knees and leaned over him. Mark didn't open his eyes.

"Mark?"

"I'm being blind," he said. Then he frowned. "I don't like it."

"Open your eyes," Jed told him, standing next to his brother.

Mark said, "I thought I knew where the base was."

"You missed it by a mile," Jed informed him.

His eyes still shut, Mark got to his feet. "Is it this way?" he asked and pointed.

"No," Jed said. He grabbed Mark and led him forward. Mark tripped. Then he began to walk with a sort of sliding shuffle, as if he were afraid to lift his feet off the ground.

He let Jed guide him to base. "Here," Jed said. Then he added, "But you're out. You ran into Stacey while she was holding the ball."

Stacey had picked up the ball (which she had dropped when Mark had collided with her) and now stood watching the brothers.

"Open your eyes," Jed repeated. He sounded a little anxious. "You're not really blind, Mark."

Mark opened his eyes. "No," he agreed.

Mark looked at Stacey. "Deb won't ever be able to see anything again," he said. "It's like she always has to walk around with her eyes closed."

Jed added, "She used to play kickball with us. Now she won't."

"She can't," Mark corrected him.

"She can't do anything now," Jed complained. "And she's mad all the time."

"Mad and sad," Mark said. His expression was serious.

"You're right," Stacey agreed, surprised at how simply and directly Mark had gotten to the heart of the matter.

"I wish Deb could still play with us," Jed said. His voice was wistful. He missed his older sister.

"I bet she wishes she could too," Stacey told him softly. "Maybe she will again someday. Just because she's blind now doesn't mean she can't do lots of things. But she has to learn new ways to do some of them."

Then Jed and Mark nodded. Stacey remembered Scout. "In fact," she said, "did you know there are special dogs that can help blind people? They're called guide dogs. Kristy and her family are raising a puppy that's going to grow up to be a guide dog. Her name is Scout."

"Is she a big dog?" Jed asked.

"What color is she?" Mark chimed in.

Stacey talked to them about dogs and guide dogs until Mrs. Cooper's car pulled into the driveway.

"Mom and Deb are back," Mark said.

Jed sprinted toward the house.

Once again, Mark and Stacey followed more slowly. They'd almost reached the back door when Mark said, "I guess it's okay for Deb to listen to the television whenever she wants."

Stacey didn't say anything. Mark opened the door. Then he said, "But you know what? I'm going to save all my money and get Deb a dog too. Maybe that would make her feel better."

"The guide dogs are — " Stacey was about to

tell him that the dogs are free, but Mark put his finger to his lips. "Shh," he said. "I want to keep it a secret until the dog gets here."

Stacey knew that getting a guide dog didn't work like that, and that Deb was too young to have one. On the other hand, Stacey knew Mark wanted to help. So Stacey said instead, "Why don't you write to the Guide Dog Foundation and ask them about guide dogs? I can get the address for you from Kristy."

"Great!" Mark exclaimed. "But remember, don't tell anyone. I want it to be a surprise."

CHAPTER 10

Although the Guide Dog Foundation offers free obedience classes every week for guide dog puppies only, the drive was too long for us. So Watson signed up Scout for a dog training class in Stoneybrook, at the community center, on Tuesday, Thursday, and Saturday afternoons. It would be okay for us to take her there, as long as we stuck to Guide Dog Foundation training rules.

It was a puppy training class, for puppies up to the age of one year. Since we couldn't bring the whole family to the class, we decided to take turns. Karen, Watson, and I went to the first class.

We arrived to find five other dogs. There were two mixed breeds. One was a large black-and-tan shepherd mix named Fender, and the other was a small white terrier mix named Riley. Then there was a rottweiler named Grace, a bull terrier named Shug, and a miniature dachshund named Britty. Scout was the youngest puppy in the class and Fender, who had just been adopted from a shelter, was the oldest. In fact, no one was sure quite how old Fender was, just that he was probably still a puppy.

The obedience trainer was a small, muscular woman named Imani. She had brown eyes, dark skin, and a brisk no-nonsense manner. She nodded when we led Scout into the small fenced-in area at the back of the center where the class was being held. She said, "Good. Good for you. What you're doing is a wonderful thing."

Karen beamed and I looked pleased. I'm not sure, but I think Watson blushed.

Imani let the dogs get acquainted with one another for a few minutes. Scout was delighted with everyone she met, even Fender, who barreled over to her in his enthusiasm. Shug kept dragging her owner around from dog to dog. I'd never seen a bull terrier before. They're strong. Britty barked at the other dogs. She was clearly a dachshund who was picky about her friends. The rottweiler, Grace, matched her name, sniffing each dog with a quiet dignity. Riley was like Scout, thrilled with everyone and everything.

As the dogs interacted, I realized that Imani was watching us and the dogs. Then she clapped her hands and asked us to line up in front of her.

"Puppies have short attention spans," she explained. "So we won't have a long class. At any rate, dog training is as much about training people as it is about training dogs. What you're going to learn is how to be a good dog trainer and owner."

Karen and I had retreated, then sat cross-legged at the edge of the line to observe. We would practice what we learned after watching the class.

I realized as I watched that reading the books Shannon and Mal had given me had helped. Imani used many of the techniques and principles I had read about.

And you know what was amazing? Imani's sit command worked the first time for every dog except the bull terrier and the dachshund, who clearly had minds of their own. Britty finally sat, but she looked like a small coiled spring about to leap into the air. When Shug, the bull terrier, eventually responded to her owner's gentle pressure, she swung her back end around so that it rested on her owner's foot.

Karen burst out laughing and several other people in the class smiled.

But Scout and Grace sat immediately — and stayed in a sitting position, almost as if they were waiting for their next command.

Imani showed the class how to teach their dogs to sit, lie down, and stay. She showed

Fender's and Shug's owners how to start working with their puppies so they didn't pull on their leashes. Then she told us to be sure to have at least two short practice sessions a day with what we had learned until the next class.

As soon as the class was over, Karen ran to Scout. "You are the smartest puppy in the whole world," she said. Then she looked up at Imani, who had joined us. "I'm going to be a dog trainer," she announced.

Karen's ambitions are wide-ranging and change often, so I wasn't surprised by her latest career plans. Imani nodded seriously and said, "I started training my first dog when I was about your age. Her name was Tinker and she was the best dog I've ever had."

"Is it hard?" Karen asked.

Imani thought about it for a moment, then said, "It's hard work sometimes but never dull. Every dog is different." She stroked Scout's head. "I like working with these guys. They have been responsibly bred and they're usually some of the easiest dogs to train."

"She gets more special training when she goes back to the guide dog school," Karen said.

Just then, we heard a yelp and then a roar of barking and snarling and snapping. Startled, I looked around to see that Britty had launched herself at Fender.

84

Imani moved quickly. She caught Britty's leash and pulled her back in midspring. Fender's owner already had a tight grip on Fender and was keeping him away. As if she had eyes in the back of her head, Imani spun around and stepped in front of Shug, who was dragging her owner at top speed toward the brouhaha, determined to join in.

"Oh, no, you don't," she said to Shug, giving the leash a quick snap and bringing Shug to a halt.

Shug immediately sat down and looked up at Imani innocently.

"Look," said Karen. "Fender is afraid of Britty!"

It was true. The big shepherd puppy was pressed against his owner's shins, his tail tucked between his legs, while Britty, now several yards away, continued to growl softly.

"I'm sorry," Britty's owner gasped. "She's like that sometimes."

"No problem," said Imani. "In the next class we'll talk about dog interactions and socialization. That means training your dog to get along with other dogs."

I glanced down at Scout. She was standing, staring at the other dogs, but she wasn't growling or pulling on her leash. "Good girl," I whispered. I knew then that Scout was going to be a wonderful guide dog.

CHAPTER 11

I was startled when Deb answered the door when I arrived for my afternoon baby-sitting job.

"Uh, hi, Deb," I said. Then I added, "It's me. Kristy."

Deb raised her hand to touch her dark glasses and said, "Duh. Come in."

She stepped back. Her welcome was not the most gracious one I've ever received, but what could I say? The last time I had seen her was on the day of my disastrous visitor idea. "Thank you," I said with a calm politeness that would have impressed Mary Anne. And since it is polite to ask, I continued, "How are you?"

Wrong question.

Scowling, Deb replied, "How do you think? Blind, thank you."

She turned and walked down the hall, her hands outstretched slightly in front of her.

Jed came bounding into the hall. "We got a

new play set. It has a sliding board shaped like a dinosaur! Come see!"

He raced away and Mr. Cooper appeared. I felt dizzy for a moment, as if I were on the set of a play in which the actors keep entering and exiting from every direction.

"Hi, Mr. Cooper," I said.

"Kristy, how are you doing?" he asked.

"Fine," I told him. "I hear you have a dinosaur in your backyard."

He laughed. "Yes. That's where you'll be spending most of your afternoon. Mrs. Cooper had to go into New York for a conference today, as you know. I'm going to pick her up at the station and then we're going to do some errands. We'll be home by five-thirty. Mark and Jed are in the backyard, and Deb is in the den, with the television on."

I nodded and said, "And your list of where to reach you is on the counter by the phone in the kitchen?"

"Mm-hm. Well, I'd better get going." With a wave and a jingle of his car keys, Mr. Cooper was gone.

I stopped in the den and said, "Deb, do you want to come out into the backyard? It's a beautiful day."

She shrugged. But to my surprise, she also clicked off the TV with the remote and stood up. "I want to go to the video store," she said.

"There's nothing to listen to on television. I want to listen to some new movies."

"Maybe we can do that," I said. "Let's go see if Mark and Jed want to go to the video store."

Deb sighed as if asking her brothers was the biggest pain in the world. I had to smile. Her reaction sounded like a fairly typical big-sister response. Maybe, I thought, she was beginning to adjust to what had happened.

Boy, was I wrong!

Since I'm a fast learner, I didn't offer to help Deb find her way to the backyard. Instead, I just kept talking as I headed, not too quickly, in that direction.

She followed me slowly, stopping to grope for the back steps with her outstretched foot. She didn't respond to anything I said and she let the back door slam hard behind her.

Mark and Jed looked up. Jed shouted excitedly, "Deb! Hey, Deb!"

"I can hear fine," Deb said. "I'm blind, not deaf."

"Take it easy, Deb," I said mildly.

She ignored me.

"Come play with our new swings," Mark said.

"The slide is shaped like a dinosaur," Jed added. "It's cool."

"Very cool," I agreed. It was a new swing set

with a slide at one end. The boys climbed up the front of the dinosaur and over its shoulder, and slid down the slide which curved along its back and tail.

"Come try it," Jed urged.

"Come on," I said to Deb.

She took a few steps out into the yard and stopped. Mark jumped off the bottom of the slide and ran toward her. He slid his hand into hers and tugged. "Come on. I'll show you how. It's easy."

Deb turned her face down toward his voice. She seemed to be considering the possibility.

"I'm going to give it a try," I told her and climbed up the dinosaur steps as Jed shrieked with delight.

I slid down and shouted as I reached the bottom.

"That's great," I said.

"I know," Jed replied and hurled himself after me.

I looked up, hoping to see that Deb had joined us. But she hadn't moved, and as I watched, she pulled her hand free of Mark's. "I don't want to slide on a sliding board," she said. "I want to go to the video store."

"No-o-o," wailed Jed. "Our dinosaur just got here."

"Can't we keep playing? Please?" Mark begged.

"Maybe we'll go a little later, Deb. How does that sound?" I asked.

"I want to go now," Deb insisted.

"In a little while," I told her.

"Fine!" Deb snapped. "Be as selfish as you want. I'll just sit in the dark in the den until you're ready." She turned and walked back to the house. I held my breath, afraid she would trip over the stairs. But I was also afraid to help her.

Not only did she make it through, but she managed to slam the door behind her.

"I'll be right back," I said to Jed and Mark. "Stay here."

I went into the house after Deb. She had already returned to her now-familiar position in the chair near the television.

"Deb, we'll go in a little while," I assured her. "Why don't you stay outside with us?"

In answer, she picked up the remote control and clicked on the television.

I went to the window and raised it slightly. The window looked out onto the backyard. "I've opened the window," I told her. "If you need anything, just call."

She didn't answer. I left her sitting in the chair, staring into space behind her dark glasses.

Although I didn't think Deb could get into any trouble sitting in the den, I checked on her several times while we were swinging and sliding. She hadn't moved. After the first couple of times, when I spoke to her through the window and she ignored me, I didn't speak.

At a quarter to four, we trooped back inside. "Deb," I said as we hurried down the hall. "Are you ready to go to the video store now? Because we . . ." My voice trailed off.

Deb wasn't in her chair. The television was no longer on.

"Deb?" I said to the empty den.

"Maybe she's in her room," Mark said.

"Or the bathroom," Jed suggested.

But she wasn't in either place.

Suddenly I had a very bad feeling.

Deb Cooper was missing.

CHAPTER 12

Don't panic, I told myself. *A good baby-sitter doesn't panic.*

"We'll check the entire house," I told Jed and Mark. "Just to be sure. Deb could be hiding."

"Hide-and-seek!" Jed said. He ran up the stairs with Mark behind him.

I did a quick check of all the downstairs closets. I even looked in the walk-in pantry in the kitchen. But Deb wasn't there.

I ran upstairs to find Mark and Jed dodging from one room to another, throwing open closet doors and looking under beds calling, "Deb, Deb, where are you?"

They still thought it was a game.

To begin my search of the upstairs I went into a room at the other end of the hall and paused by a window. A movement far down the street caught my eye.

Squinting, I tried to remember what Deb had been wearing: a red cotton sweatshirt and jeans.

The figure moved, then stopped. It was wearing jeans and something red.

It was Deb.

"Mark! Jed!" I called, dashing into the hall.

They poked their heads out of Jed's bedroom. I thought fast. "Hide somewhere in your bedroom, Jed, or in Mark's, and count to five hundred. Then wait and I'll come find you."

"Hide-and-seek!" Jed sang out again, and the boys disappeared into Jed's room as I raced out of the house in the direction where I had seen Deb.

As I ran, I saw Deb stop again and turn. She was clearly disoriented and confused. She took another step, then another. She stumbled off the curb and took three quick steps to regain her balance. I yelled out to her, but I don't think she heard me.

She had walked into the middle of the street.

I stifled a cry as I saw the light turn red. Deb was safe for the moment — as long as she didn't move out of the crosswalk.

She moved forward. She stepped out of the bright painted lines and into the traffic.

Someone honked. A second horn joined in.

A woman leaned out of her window and said, "Hey, kid, watch where you're going! You'll get hurt!"

Deb jumped back.

I sprinted into the intersection and grabbed

her arm. She leaped into the air as if I had shouted "Boo!"

"Deb, it's me," I said, fighting to keep the panic out of my voice. "Come on."

She grabbed my arm with both hands, but she didn't move.

The light changed. Horns blared.

"Deb, turn and walk with me," I ordered. "We're in the middle of the street and we need to walk back to the sidewalk."

Her grip on my arm tightened painfully. But she turned as I did and began to walk — no, shuffle — back to the curb.

Some of the horns stopped, as if the people inside the cars realized that it wasn't helping. Still, it seemed to take forever for us to reach the side of the street.

"Step up for the curb," I said. "Okay, now walk forward. Good. We're on the sidewalk."

Dimly, I heard the cars begin to whoosh past behind me. I realized that my knees were shaking. I wanted to scream.

Instead, I kept my voice calm as I said, "Deb, what were you doing?"

"Go — go —" She took a deep breath and swallowed. "Going to the video store."

"Well, you were going in the wrong direction," I said, my voice rising in spite of myself. "You could have been killed."

I was harsher than I'd intended to be, because I was still scared. It made me feel sick to think about what could have happened.

"Maybe that wouldn't have been so . . . so . . . bad. . . ." She shook her head.

"No!" I shouted. "I mean, yes. It would have been bad. You're blind, Deb. But you still have a family, people who love you, friends who care about you — "

"Friends!" Now Deb's voice rose too. "Friends? What friends? I don't have any friends."

"Well, you haven't exactly made it easy, have you? If you treated them like you've treated me, or your family, maybe they got the idea you didn't want them around!"

"I don't want anyone feeling sorry for me," she cried furiously.

"Well, then, stop acting like someone people *should* feel sorry for! You can't change what happened, Deb. You're going to have to deal with it."

"As if *you* know about it," she shot back. "You're not blind. You can see. You can go out whenever you want. You don't need other people to help you get dressed or walk or . . ." For a moment, I thought she was going to cry. But she didn't.

We stood facing each other on the sidewalk. Then Deb did something that took me completely by surprise. She pushed her dark glasses back onto the top of her head. "Do I look funny?" she asked. "Tell me the truth."

"No," I said, and I *was* telling the truth. "You look like you. Just the same. You can lose the shades."

She thought about that for a minute, then nodded. "Maybe," she said.

She reached out her hand. "Kristy? I'd like to go home, please."

I linked my arm through hers. We walked slowly back to the house. Deb didn't speak again, but I thought about what had happened and decided that in spite of the near disaster, maybe it had been a good thing.

Deb wanted to be independent. And she understood now that she was going to have to work to get there.

When we reached the house Deb let go of my arm. "Thank you," she said. Then she added, "Don't tell Mom and Dad."

"Okay," I said. "Just this once."

Deb smiled. It was a very small smile, but it was a smile.

And at that moment, Jed popped out and shouted, "You didn't find us, Kristy! You're 'it'!"

CHAPTER 13

"Congratulations, class," Imani said, looking out at her students. Six of the students wagged their tails. The rest of us smiled.

We had finished our puppy training course. Today we would graduate. But first, Imani wanted to put us through our paces for the audience.

Audience? Yes. My family had turned out in its entirety, from Emily Michelle to Nannie. The only member missing who might also have been interested was Shannon. But we had already signed her up for the *next* class.

Although my family dominated one side of the training area, other dogs had their fans too. Fender's family (his human family) was there, and several girls were cheering Britty on. The husband of the woman who had brought Grace, the rottweiler, to class ran in late, frantically following us with his video camera.

Imani was rock-calm through it all, which seemed to calm the dogs too. She lined us up and said, "Sit." Watson said to Scout, "Sit" — and she did.

The puppies demonstrated their mastery of "Sit," "Down," and "Come," and walked in a circle on their leashes without pulling (at least, not too much). Cameras snapped and the video camera whirred. Several times, I admit, I led the crowd in applause.

Through it all, the owners of the puppies dished out lavish praise with the occasional firm, quiet "No" when a puppy didn't get a command right on the first try.

Oh, Shug, the bull terrier, still thought it was very funny to swing her behind around and sit on her person's foot on the "Sit" command, and Britty stared hard at the man with the video camera and gave him a warn-ing bark. But that didn't mean that each and every one of the puppies weren't champion A-plus, num-ber-one students.

Imani more or less said the same thing as she handed out our certificates of graduation. "You've done a good job," she told the class. "You've taken an important step toward being good, responsible dog owners. A well-trained dog can go almost anywhere, and that's the best, most loving gift you can give your dog. Congratulations!"

More applause. *Many* more pictures, including a formal class photograph taken by someone from the community center so that we could all have a copy (the community center would post the photo on the center bulletin board as well). There was also a more informal group photograph with the entire audience squeezed in.

Afterward, there were dog-shaped cookies and juice for the people, and chunks of carrot and bananas for the dogs, as well as any of the special treats that their owners had remembered to bring.

Once we'd gotten home, Watson and I took Scout out for a walk.

I looked down at her. "She did great, didn't she?" I said.

Watson nodded. "She'll be a fine guide dog someday."

I felt a sudden pang. Scout was growing up so fast. In no time at all, it would be time for her to leave us. How could we give her up? My pride in her was mingled with a sudden sadness.

I sighed. "I wish she could be a puppy forever."

I felt Watson glance at me. Then he patted my shoulder. "We won't lose track of Scout," he told me, as if he had read my thoughts. "Remember? We can even see her again, if she's placed with someone nearby, after a year has passed."

"It won't be the same," I said and sighed again.

And then something totally unexpected happened. We rounded a corner and came face-to-face with another guide dog.

But this wasn't a guide dog in training. This was a working guide dog — a regal, beautiful Labrador.

"Oh!" I exclaimed.

The young man with the guide dog turned his face toward us, giving us a questioning look.

"Um, hi," I said. "We have a guide dog too. I mean, we're puppy walkers. We have a guide dog in training. She's with us right now. Her name is Scout."

The young man stopped. His dog stopped too and stood like a rock. The man broke into a huge smile, squatted down, and reached out. "Scout?" he said.

She licked his hand and wiggled all over as he petted her.

"Toby is a Lab too," he said.

"Toby? Is that your dog's name?" I asked. I knew better than to pet Toby. When you see a guide dog at work, you shouldn't try to pet it. How would you like it if you were at work, sitting at your desk, for example, and people came up and petted you on the head all the time?

He nodded. "And my name is Jim."

"Is Toby your first guide dog?" I asked as Jim stood up again, grasping Toby's harness.

"Yes," he said. "Toby and I have been together four years. Toby's changed my life. Toby goes to the office with me, we go out to dinner, we go to movies. Together, Toby and I can do anything."

Jim told us about meeting Toby for the first time, when he went to the Guide Dog Foundation to be trained. "It was the best day of my life," he said.

We talked for a little while longer before Jim and Toby had to go. Before he left, he congratulated us for raising a puppy for the Guide Dog Foundation.

Watson and I stood and watched as Toby and Jim walked briskly and confidently away from us. I couldn't help but think of Deb, standing so lost and alone in the street, angry and scared.

Maybe one day she would have a guide dog like Toby who would change her life.

And one day Scout would change somebody else's life.

It would be hard to let Scout go, but when the time came, I could do it.

I looked up at Watson and he handed me the leash. I smiled.

"Come on, Scout," I said. "Let's go home."

CHAPTER 14

Tuesday

You know, I admire Deb's fighting spirit. Its going to go a long way toward making her independent again, once she decides to channel that energy into working with all the people who want to help her. But boy, does she still have a quick temper!

Whten Abby arrived at the Coopers' house, she discovered that Deb wasn't sitting in the den in the dark listening to the television and brooding.

"Maya is here," Mark told Abby as he led her down the hall. "She's with Deb. Maya is a mobo . . . moby . . ."

"Mobility instructor," said Mrs. Cooper. She told Abby where the list of phone numbers for emergencies was, agreed with Mark and Jed that they could have a snack before she got back, and reminded them to be sure to offer a snack to Maya if she was still there.

To Abby, Mrs. Cooper added, "As you know, Deb's been having some difficulty adjusting to what happened."

"Right," said Abby.

"So we view this as progress," Mrs. Cooper continued. "Anyway, Maya is very nice and seems quite good at what she does. I hope you get to meet her."

As soon as Mrs. Cooper left, Mark and Jed practically dragged Abby to Mark's room. "Look what I got," Mark said, holding up an envelope.

"It's a letter," Jed supplied helpfully.

"I've been checking the mail every day," Mark told Abby. "Stacey gave me the address for the dogs that help blind people, and I wrote to tell them I wanted a dog for my sister."

Sure enough, Abby saw the logo of the Guide Dog Foundation in one corner of the envelope.

Mark went on, "Will you help me read it?"

"Sure," said Abby. She sat cross-legged on the floor next to the bed with Mark on one side and Jed on the other.

" 'Dear Mark,' " she read aloud. " 'Thank you for your letter. We are glad you are interested in the Guide Dog Foundation. You asked how much a guide dog would cost for your sister. The guide dogs at this time cost over twenty thousand dollars to train — ' "

"Twenty thousand dollars!" Mark gasped. "I can never save up that much money!"

"You can have my piggy bank," Jed offered.

"Wait," Abby interrupted gently. "There's more. '. . . but they are free to the people who need them. We ask that a person who is going to work with our guide dogs come to live in the dormitory at our foundation for approximately three weeks to learn how to work with a guide dog, and we like for guide dog owners to be at least sixteen years old. We have placed guide dogs all over the world.

" 'We hope you will come visit the Guide Dog Foundation. Enclosed is a brochure with more information.' "

When Abby finished the letter, Mark said

glumly, "It'll be years before Deb is old enough to have her own guide dog."

"When she's sixteen," Abby said. "That's not *so* long. I think your idea is a wonderful one, Mark."

"You do?" Mark asked, looking a little less upset.

"Yes, I do."

Just then, they heard a thump in the hall and an angry exclamation. "Who put that there?!" Deb cried. "I'll never get this. It's stupid!"

Naturally, Abby followed Mark and Jed out into the hall to see what was going on.

Deb was standing outside the door of her room, awkwardly holding onto a long white cane with a red tip. Beside her was a young woman with a friendly face and kind eyes, who said in an unruffled tone, "It does seem stupid at first. But with practice, you'll get the hang of it."

"Hi, Maya," Jed said.

Maya glanced in the direction of Abby and the Cooper boys. "Hi," she said.

Abby said, "We haven't met. I'm Abby Stevenson. I'm here to sit with Mark and Jed."

Jed blurted out, "And guess what, Deb? You can have a guide dog instead of a cane someday. When you're sixteen!"

That got Deb's attention. She frowned in

Jed's direction and said, "What are you talking about?"

"I wrote to the guide dog place and they wrote me back, all about guide dogs. They're free!" Mark explained.

"We were about to have a snack," Abby told Deb and Maya. "Do you want to join us?"

"Thanks," Maya said before Deb could answer. "We will. You go on to the kitchen. We'll be right there."

They didn't arrive right away. But when Maya and Deb came into the kitchen, it seemed to Abby that Deb was already moving around in her new world with a little more confidence.

Abby put out juice and oatmeal-raisin cookies, while Maya talked in a general way about what a mobility instructor does. "Basically, I teach a person to get oriented," she explained. "To develop an inner compass to help him or her navigate in the world and handle any obstacles that might arise."

Although Maya was talking to all of them, Abby could sense that what she was saying was largely directed at Deb. After a while, Deb said, "Maybe a guide dog wouldn't be so bad."

Mark said, "Kristy has one!"

Startled, Deb said, "Kristy? But she's not blind!"

"Kristy is a baby-sitter too," Abby told

Maya. She went on to explain how my family had become volunteers to raise a guide dog puppy until it was old enough to go into training to be a guide dog.

"Scout — that's their puppy's name — just finished a puppy obedience class," Abby said. Now it was her turn to tell stories about Scout and the guide dog program. Deb seemed interested. Maybe, Abby thought, it would give her more hope.

As they finished their snacks, Maya said, "It's time for me to go." She stood up and said, "Deb, why don't you walk me to the front door?"

Deb made a face, but she didn't argue. As they left the kitchen, Abby heard Maya say, "You know, before you can get a guide dog, you'll have to learn basic orientation. If you don't know how to get to where you're going, how can you tell your dog?"

"I get the point," Deb answered tartly. But Abby didn't think she sounded quite so cross.

Abby looked at Mark and Jed. "You know what?" she said. "Not only was your idea a great one, Mark, but I predict that someday soon, Deb will be booking through the world with a guide dog of her own."

CHAPTER 15

Abby was telling us about her sitting job with the Coopers, and I was rifling through my pack when I had an idea. And this time, it was a truly brilliant idea.

"Puppy Walker Fun Day!" I exclaimed, rudely interrupting Abby.

Abby's used to me. She raised one eyebrow and waited.

Claudia said, "An idea, President Thomas?"

"An idea," I agreed. "We've been invited to Puppy Walker Fun Day at the Guide Dog Foundation. It's a celebration to honor all the puppy walkers, past and present."

"That's so nice," said Jessi as I pulled one of the invitations out of my pack.

Waving the invitation in the air, I said, "It's the perfect opportunity."

"For what?" Stacey asked.

Mal plucked the invitation from my hand before I could answer and said, "Look at this.

There's a costume parade for the dogs. And a family tree, so you can see your dog's family history. And refreshments."

"Perfect opportunity for what?" Stacey repeated.

"For Deb. For the Coopers. I'm going to invite them to go with us."

Mary Anne said, "Kristy! You're right. It's the perfect opportunity. *And* it's a brilliant idea."

"If you can convince Deb," Jessi cautioned me.

"I'll convince her," I said. "Trust me."

Abby burst out laughing. "You will, Kristy. You will. Deb doesn't stand a chance!"

Surprisingly, Deb didn't take as much convincing as I thought she would. And so, on Puppy Walker Fun Day we returned to the Guide Dog Foundation. My whole family was there, plus the Coopers, plus an enormous, beautiful butterfly.

Butterfly? Yup. Scout was wearing a pair of amazing cardboard butterfly wings attached to a harness that had been covered with material to look like a butterfly body.

Naturally, we had Claudia to thank for this. She'd measured Scout and figured out how to make the outfit. Amazingly enough, Scout was wearing the costume as if it were a part of her.

Deb was nervous about being among so many people. But it didn't last long, especially not with Karen there to ask questions.

"Hi," she would call. "How old is your dog? What's her name? Have you raised many puppies? This is Scout. She's a butterfly. She's our first guide dog puppy. We have a puppy named Shannon and we had a dog named Louie. . . ."

We met one woman, a retired schoolteacher, who had raised seventeen guide dog puppies. Through her puppies she had made friends all over the world. I was reassured to hear that she stayed in touch with most of the people who had dogs she'd raised. Her current puppy, who wasn't much older than Scout, was dressed as a dalmatian!

We saw dogs dressed as sunflowers and superheros (which, in my opinion, all the dogs are), princesses and angels. One dog was even dressed up in a carrot outfit, complete with a feathery green hat to represent the stalk. A few people were raising more than one puppy. One man had a golden retriever who had not completed guide dog training after it was discovered she had a hip problem. Since that might have meant problems for her future owner, she was taken out of the program. He'd welcomed her back into the family with open arms, and now she was the dog mentor to the guide dog puppies the man continued to raise.

Jed and Mark talked almost as much as Karen, and among them, the Coopers kept Deb posted on all the activity around her. She stooped to feel the feathery top on the carrot-dog costume and actually laughed when her father told her about the "dalmatian."

Then the younger kids spotted the obstacle course set up for the dogs to climb over and under and through. Naturally, they didn't think it was just for dogs. With Charlie and Nannie trailing behind them, they ran to try it out.

Just then I saw Gillian. I waved her over to us. "Kristy," she said, "we're glad you could make it."

"I am too," I told her. I introduced Deb, who immediately held out her hand and waited for Gillian to take it.

As they shook hands, Deb said, "I hope I can have a guide dog someday."

"That would be great," said Gillian.

"I'm going to ask for a chocolate Lab, just like Scout," Deb went on.

"It's possible that you might even have one of Scout's younger brothers or sisters, or a cousin," Gillian answered. "Most of our dogs are bred and raised right here."

We glanced at Scout. Nannie was holding her butterfly wings as she followed Karen and David Michael through a large tunnel that had been set up as part of the obstacle course. As usual, Scout was wagging her tail as hard as she could.

Just then, Mark came hurrying back to us. He grabbed Deb by the hand. "Deb," he said, "they're taking pictures of the dogs in their costumes. Come have your picture taken with Scout."

"I think we should all have our picture taken together," I said. Then I waited, holding my breath.

For a moment, Deb looked uncertain. Then she lifted her chin and shrugged. "Why not?"

In case you think it's easy to squeeze all those people plus one dog in a butterfly costume into a photograph — it's not. It reminded me of the stunt in which as many people as possible try to squeeze into a phone booth.

But we finally did it. It's a great photograph. We fill up every available inch of space on it. Karen has her mouth open, talking. David Michael and Andrew are laughing at what she's saying. Watson and Mom have their arms linked, and Emily Michelle is resting on Nannie's hip. Charlie has his eyes closed and Sam has one hand raised as if he's about to wave.

Jed and Mark are crouched in front, grinning broadly.

Deb is standing between her parents, who are smiling too, each resting a hand on one of her shoulders.

Deb isn't smiling. But she's staring straight out at the camera — without her dark glasses — as if she can see a little bit into a future that looks all right.

And Scout, with her mouth open and her tongue hanging out in a dog grin, is the most beautiful of all.

I'm going to make a copy of that picture and put it up in my room next to a poster I got the first time I visited the foundation. It shows a guide dog in a harness beneath a caption that reads "Sit. Stay. See."

Scout has a long way to go, just like Deb, but I know they're both going to make it. And maybe I'll raise other puppies for the foundation and send them out into the world to make it a better place.

I'll visit them, too.

Who knows — maybe I'll even write a book about it.

GuideDog Foundation
For The Blind, Inc.®

The Guide Dog Foundation for the Blind, Inc.® was founded in 1946 to provide guide dogs free of charge to blind people who seek enhanced independence and mobility.

A fully trained guide dog, on-campus training, transportation to and from the Foundation, and a comprehensive after care program, if needed, are offered at no cost to the blind student. At the present time, there are over 350 Foundation teams working in 47 states and 5 foreign countries.

If you'd like to know more about the Guide Dog Foundation for the Blind, you can call 1-800-548-4337 or 516-265-2121. You can also write to 371 East Jericho Turnpike, Smithtown, New York, 11787, or E-mail *guidedog@guidedog.org*. Plus, you can check out the Foundation website at *http//www.guidedog.org* on the World Wide Web.

Dear Reader,

In *Kristy Thomas, Dog Trainer*, Kristy's family takes on a big responsibility when they agree to train a guide dog. Training a guide dog is a *huge* commitment. Kristy's family has to be very careful about what they teach Scout, where they take her, and how they let her behave. When Scout grows up, she's going to have a lot of responsibility, so it's extra important that the Thomases train her well.

Training any pet is a big responsibility. It takes lots of patience. Right now, I am training my new cat, Willy, not to claw the furniture. This is a slow process, but he is learning. He is also learning not to take Gussie's and Woody's food. Every day he gets a little better, and I reward him for good behavior.

When you're training a pet, remember the three P's — practice, perseverance, and patience!

Happy reading,

Ann M Martin

Ann M. Martin

About the Author

ANN MATTHEWS MARTIN was born on August 12, 1955. She grew up in Princeton, NJ, with her parents and her younger sister, Jane.

Although Ann used to be a teacher and then an editor of children's books, she's now a full-time writer. She gets the ideas for her books from many different places. Some are based on personal experiences. Others are based on childhood memories and feelings. Many are written about contemporary problems or events.

All of Ann's characters, even the members of the Baby-sitters Club, are made up. (So is Stoneybrook.) But many of her characters are based on real people. Sometimes Ann names her characters after people she knows; other times she chooses names she likes.

In addition to the Baby-sitters Club books, Ann Martin has written many other books for children. Her favorite is *Ten Kids, No Pets* because she loves big families and she loves animals. Her favorite Baby-sitters Club book is *Kristy's Big Day*. (By the way, Kristy is her favorite baby-sitter!)

Ann M. Martin now lives in New York with her cats, Gussie, Woody, and Willy. Her hobbies are reading, sewing, and needlework — especially making clothes for children.

Notebook Pages

This Baby-sitters Club book belongs to _____.

I am _____ years old and in the _____

grade.

The name of my school is _____.

I got this BSC book from _____.

I started reading it on _____ and

finished reading it on _____.

The place where I read most of this book is _____.

My favorite part was when _____.

If I could change anything in the story, it might be the part when

_____

My favorite character in the Baby-sitters Club is _____.

The BSC member I am most like is _____

because _____.

If I could write a Baby-sitters Club book it would be about _____

_____.

#118 Kristy Thomas, Dog Trainer

Kristy is very excited about training Scout to be a guide dog. If my family was training a guide dog, we'd need to find a place for her to sleep. I'd like her to sleep in _____.

Kristy is very excited to show Scout to her friends in the BSC. I would want to show my new dog to _____

_____. As part of Scout's training, Kristy takes her to Krushers practice, BSC meetings, and the supermarket. If I were training a guide dog, I would take her to _____

_____. One place I would *not* take her is _____. Kristy loves Scout's name, since Scout is also the name of a character in *To Kill a Mockingbird*, which is one of Kristy's favorite books. If I had a new dog, I would name him/her _____. I like this name because _____

_____.

KRISTY'S

Playing softball with some of my favorite sitting charges.

A gab-fest

Me, age 3. Already on the go.

SCRAPBOOK

n mary Anne!

My family keeps growing!

David Michael, me, and
Louie — the best dog ever.

Illustrations by Angelo Tillery

Read all the books
about **Kristy**
in the Baby-sitters Club series
by Ann M. Martin

THE BABY-SITTERS CLUB

Look for #119

STACEY'S EX-BOYFRIEND

"Are you sure you two aren't getting back together?" Abby pressed.

"Positive," I insisted. Although, truthfully, I didn't feel sure about anything that was going on between us. I cared about Robert, but I no longer felt the way I used to feel. I just wanted to help.

If only I could understand what had gone wrong with him. I remembered Claudia's theory — that he'd broken off with me because something had started bothering him at that time. It made sense. But what was it that bothered him so? Why couldn't he work up any enthusiasm for anything?

That night I couldn't fall asleep because I couldn't stop thinking about Robert, wondering what was bugging him. It was a problem I had to solve. I was involved now. I couldn't back off the way I had done in February.

If Robert liked talking to me, then it made sense that I should spend as much time as possible talking to him. Robert had always stood by me when I had problems. When I didn't make the cheerleading squad, he quit the basketball team to be supportive. I talked his ear off when I was deciding whether or not to stay in the BSC, back in that disastrous time when I quit for awhile. No matter what my problem was, Robert had always been there for me.

Now it was my turn. I owed him that much.

THE BABY-SITTERS CLUB®

Collect 'em all!

100 (and more) Reasons to Stay Friends Forever!

More

The Baby-sitters Club titles continued...

❑ MG22880-3	#96	**Abby's Lucky Thirteen**	$3.99
❑ MG22881-1	#97	**Claudia and the World's Cutest Baby**	$3.99
❑ MG22882-X	#98	**Dawn and Too Many Sitters**	$3.99
❑ MG69205-4	#99	**Stacey's Broken Heart**	$3.99
❑ MG69206-2	#100	**Kristy's Worst Idea**	$3.99
❑ MG69207-0	#101	**Claudia Kishi, Middle School Dropout**	$3.99
❑ MG69208-9	#102	**Mary Anne and the Little Princess**	$3.99
❑ MG69209-7	#103	**Happy Holidays, Jessi**	$3.99
❑ MG69210-0	#104	**Abby's Twin**	$3.99
❑ MG69211-9	#105	**Stacey the Math Whiz**	$3.99
❑ MG69212-7	#106	**Claudia, Queen of the Seventh Grade**	$3.99
❑ MG69213-5	#107	**Mind Your Own Business, Kristy!**	$3.99
❑ MG69214-3	#108	**Don't Give Up, Mallory**	$3.99
❑ MG69215-1	#109	**Mary Anne to the Rescue**	$3.99
❑ MG05988-2	#110	**Abby the Bad Sport**	$3.99
❑ MG05989-0	#111	**Stacey's Secret Friend**	$3.99
❑ MG05990-4	#112	**Kristy and the Sister War**	$3.99
❑ MG05911-2	#113	**Claudia Makes Up Her Mind**	$3.99
❑ MG05911-2	#114	**The Secret Life of Mary Anne Spier**	$3.99
❑ MG05993-9	#115	**Jessi's Big Break**	$3.99
❑ MG05994-7	#116	**Abby and the Worst Kid Ever**	$3.99
❑ MG05995-5	#117	**Claudia and the Terrible Truth**	$3.99
❑ MG05996-3	#118	**Kristy Thomas, Dog Trainer**	$3.99
❑ MG45575-3		**Logan's Story Special Edition Readers' Request**	$3.25
❑ MG47118-X		**Logan Bruno, Boy Baby-sitter**	
		Special Edition Readers' Request	$3.50
❑ MG47756-0		**Shannon's Story Special Edition Reader's Request**	$3.50
❑ MG47686-6		**The Baby-sitters Club Guide to Baby-sitting**	$3.25
❑ MG47314-X		**The Baby-sitters Club Trivia and Puzzle Fun Book**	$2.50
❑ MG48400-1		**BSC Portrait Collection: Claudia's Book**	$3.50
❑ MG22864-1		**BSC Portrait Collection: Dawn's Book**	$3.50
❑ MG69181-3		**BSC Portrait Collection: Kristy's Book**	$3.99
❑ MG22865-X		**BSC Portrait Collection: Mary Anne's Book**	$3.99
❑ MG48399-4		**BSC Portrait Collection: Stacey's Book**	$3.50
❑ MG69182-1		**BSC Portrait Collection: Abby's Book**	$3.99
❑ MG92713-2		**The Complete Guide to The Baby-sitters Club**	$4.95
❑ MG47151-1		**The Baby-sitters Club Chain Letter**	$14.95
❑ MG48295-5		**The Baby-sitters Club Secret Santa**	$14.95
❑ MG45074-3		**The Baby-sitters Club Notebook**	$2.50
❑ MG44783-1		**The Baby-sitters Club Postcard Book**	$4.95

Available wherever you buy books...or use this order form.

THE BABY-SITTERS CLUB

by Ann M. Martin

Collect and read these exciting BSC Super Specials, Mysteries, and Super Mysteries along with your favorite Baby-sitters Club books!

BSC Super Specials

BSC Mysteries

More titles ➡

The Baby-sitters Club books continued...

❏ BAI47050-7	#12 Dawn and the Surfer Ghost	$3.50
❏ BAI47051-5	#13 Mary Anne and the Library Mystery	$3.50
❏ BAI47052-3	#14 Stacey and the Mystery at the Mall	$3.50
❏ BAI47053-1	#15 Kristy and the Vampires	$3.50
❏ BAI47054-X	#16 Claudia and the Clue in the Photograph	$3.99
❏ BAI48232-7	#17 Dawn and the Halloween Mystery	$3.50
❏ BAI48233-5	#18 Stacey and the Mystery at the Empty House	$3.50
❏ BAI48234-3	#19 Kristy and the Missing Fortune	$3.50
❏ BAI48309-9	#20 Mary Anne and the Zoo Mystery	$3.50
❏ BAI48310-2	#21 Claudia and the Recipe for Danger	$3.50
❏ BAI22866-8	#22 Stacey and the Haunted Masquerade	$3.50
❏ BAI22867-6	#23 Abby and the Secret Society	$3.99
❏ BAI22868-4	#24 Mary Anne and the Silent Witness	$3.99
❏ BAI22869-2	#25 Kristy and the Middle School Vandal	$3.99
❏ BAI22870-6	#26 Dawn Schafer, Undercover Baby-sitter	$3.99
❏ BAI69175-9	#27 Claudia and the Lighthouse Ghost	$3.99
❏ BAI69176-7	#28 Abby and the Mystery Baby	$3.99
❏ BAI69177-5	#29 Stacey and the Fashion Victim	$3.99
❏ BAI69178-3	#30 Kristy and the Mystery Train	$3.99
❏ BAI69179-1	#31 Mary Anne and the Music Box Secret	$3.99
❏ BAI05972-6	#32 Claudia and the Mystery in the Painting	$3.99
❏ BAI05973-4	#33 Stacey and the Stolen Hearts	$3.99

BSC Super Mysteries

❏ BAI48311-0	Super Mystery #1: Baby-sitters' Haunted House	$3.99
❏ BAI22871-4	Super Mystery #2: Baby-sitters Beware	$3.99
❏ BAI69180-5	Super Mystery #3: Baby-sitters' Fright Night	$4.50
❏ BAI69180-5	Super Mystery #4: Baby-sitters' Christmas Chiller	$4.50

Available wherever you buy books...or use this order form.

Scholastic Inc., P.O. Box 7502, 2931 East McCarty Street, Jefferson City, MO 65102-7502

Please send me the books I have checked above. I am enclosing $ _____
(please add $2.00 to cover shipping and handling). Send check or money order
— no cash or C.O.D.s please.

Name_____Birthdate_____

Address _____

City_____State/Zip_____

allow four to six weeks for delivery. Offer good in the U.S. only. Sorry, mail orders are not
to residents of Canada. Prices subject to change.